Higamus, Hogamus

by Pierre Parisien

Note for Librarians: A cataloguing record for this book is available from Library and Archives Canada at www.collectionscanada.ca/amicus/index-e.html

ISBN 1-4120-6563-1

Printed on paper with minimum 30% recycled fibre. Trafford's print shop runs on "green energy" from solar, wind and other environmentally-friendly power sources.

Offices in Canada, USA, Ireland and UK
This book was published *on-demand* in cooperation with Trafford Publishing. On-demand publishing is a unique process and service of making a book available for retail sale to the public taking advantage of on-demand manufacturing and Internet marketing. On-demand publishing includes promotions, retail sales, manufacturing, order fulfilment, accounting and collecting royalties on behalf of the author.

Book sales for North America and international:
Trafford Publishing, 6E–2333 Government St.,
Victoria, BC V8T 4P4 CANADA
phone 250 383 6864 (toll-free 1 888 232 4444)
fax 250 383 6804; email to orders@trafford.com
Book sales in Europe:
Trafford Publishing (UK) Limited, 9 Park End Street, 2nd Floor
Oxford, UK OX1 1HH UNITED KINGDOM
phone 44 (0)1865 722 113 (local rate 0845 230 9601)
facsimile 44 (0)1865 722 868; info.uk@trafford.com
Order online at:
trafford.com/05-1474

10 9 8 7 6 5 4 3 2

I

He had not intended it; had not expected it; had not even thought about it. He left his hotel room because he was bored and restless, and because Nerve was in one of its frequent unstable states, unable to choose between a double martini or a quest for adventure and excitement. (He often slipped into such moods whenever he attended those dumb social work seminars. This one, *Social Workers and the Challenge of the 70's* was even more boring than most.) He started walking east on Boylston Street and upon reaching Massachusetts Avenue he suddenly remembered that during his college days at Boston College he had often noticed streetwalkers on that particular street.

(Of course, he had not availed himself of their services. Those were the innocent days, the days before the onset of terminal moral decrepitude – *decripitudis moralis* – that insidious disease whose virus seemed to infect the very waters of River and from which none seemed immune but a certain rare type of madman.

Well, that was the way River flowed and nothing much could be done about it.)

But enough! Right then, River had brought him to the corner of Boylston and Massachusetts Avenue and there were whores in them thar hills, with funky bushes, and he was going to walk the gauntlet and suffer the slings and arrows of blunt propositions – "Going out tonight, baby?' "How about it, honey?" "Hey handsome, where you rushing to?" – and he was going to say, "No thanks, not tonight, baby," or "Honey you look gorgeous and I would just love to, but I just don't have the bread," and he was going to emerge unscathed and only slightly titillated.

And he walked down Massachusetts Avenue and the whores, on cue, asked, "Going out tonight, baby?" and he replied, "No thanks, not tonight, baby," and he walked with that same second-string-running-back swagger he had adopted at Boston College and he felt, for a few minutes, like he was back in school, back on the football field, back at the wild dorm parties.

But then he tripped, and what tripped him was not an outrageous cleavage or an oversized pair of false eyelashes. What tripped him was a warm soothing voice that, sensing a certain stress in the way his body and eyes had responded to its proposition, said, "It's okay, baby, you don't have to. You don't have to." He had little experience with prostitutes, but being treated as a brother human, rather than a customer, by one of them seemed unusual. He sensed a certain generous refusal to take advantage of any vulnerability on his part and, without hesitation, he smiled and said, "Why not?" forgetting that he had not intended it.

"I'm Felicia. What's your name?"

"Jerome. Jerome Dubinski."

"You a communist?"

"Hell no! Do I look like a communist?"

"No, It's just that Dubinski sounds like a communist name. But I was only kidding."

"Dubinski is Polish, but I don't even speak it. My mother's Irish and I think I'm more Irish than Polish – American, that's what I am, I guess."

"I'm Cherokee – mostly. And a little everything else – French, Black..."

"Hey, by the way, I don't have too much money on me."

"You got twenty? You look like a nice guy. We

can use my place, which I don't usually do, you know. That way, you save four bucks."

"All right. And, hey, I like you too."

"Good. We'll have a good time. You see."

She walked just a foot or so ahead of him as though guiding him through unfamiliar territory and he had a chance to look her over: a slim, tallish girl in her twenties, fairly athletic looking, but with a tired and used aura about her. Her pleasant, smiling face did look slightly Indian, but perhaps that was due to a headband which bisected the area between her eyes and her hair line.

She slowed down and allowed him to catch up with her. Suddenly, she took his hand in hers and that sad half-smile that seemed permanently etched on her face simultaneously brightened, and she then gently pulled him into a ninety-degree turn and led him into a red brick tenement and up a dark staircase, and he found himself alone with her in a sparsely furnished but clean and comfortable room that was suffused by the dim reddish glow of a naked bulb, hanging from the ceiling.

From her first warm smile on Massachusetts Avenue he had known that this would be unlike his two or three previous experiences with prostitutes. Whereas, on those occasions, he had undressed silently – and the woman likewise – furtively glancing at the progressively exposed flesh from the corner of his eyes – as though a preview of coming attractions was not included in the price of admission – all the while hoping that the unveiling would be complete (he disliked whores who, in their quest for greater productivity, wanted to undress only partially), this time the disrobing was slow and deliberate, as though part of a ritual. They talked, calling each other by their first name, and smiled and she allowed him to unfasten her bra. His fingers stumbled for a moment, as they always did, trying to find their way in the small jungle of hooks and eyes, but then the two ends of the bra separated and he let it fall to her feet while his hands rounded the curve of her rib cage until he cupped them gently around her breasts. He had noticed then that her flesh felt soft and yielding, as though her skin was just a half size larger than the rest of her body – not enough to look wrinkled, but enough to create a pleasant and sensuous looseness.

"I like the way your titties feel."

"I like the way your hands feel."

"We're going to have a go-o-o-d time."

"Huh-huh."

He kissed the nape of her neck and rolled her nipples between his thumbs and forefingers. He looked down over her shoulder and saw how long and dark-hued those nipples were and how they transformed her otherwise modest and unprepossessing breasts into potent erotic weapons. He let his hands travel over the contour of her body until he reached her panties and, with barely a guiding impulse, they slipped off, as though of their own accord. Gently, but unhesitatingly, he pulled her down as he fell upon the bed, then, in one movement he rolled over, landing on her body with his mouth already enclosing most of her left breast, his tongue circumnavigating the mountainside of her erected nipple.

When he had eaten his fill of tit, he let his tongue climb down to her belly button, stopping in that musty oasis just long enough to savor the salinity of her skin – obviously the physical demands of her trade had made her sweat previously – then, journeying down toward the magic mountain with its smoking crater hidden beneath its dark and tangled forest, he came across an area whose topography both startled and intrigued him: ravaged by a previous pregnancy and childbirth, Felicia's lower abdomen was crisscrossed by a grid of deep furrows and wide stretch-marks. At first, it turned him off somewhat but, inexplicably, this wound, caused by the biological shackles that are the curse and the blessing of all females, had suddenly sent him into an erotic frenzy and his lips, teeth and tongue engaged in a furious exploration of this strange domain. Her skin, which, as he had noticed before, was soft and loose, was even more so there and he was able to suck in large wads of flesh into his mouth and was chewing on this cud contentedly when Felicia, her hand gently pushing down on his head, reminded him of his duty. Penitently, he dragged his head a few inches south and, forgetting that she was a whore and that there was no telling what balance of her previous transactions remained on deposit, placed his hands under her buttocks in order to raise her offering to a more accessible level and, after untangling her pubic hair with a few expert sweeps of his tongue, he made contact with her already blood-congested clitoris.

At first he had been content to merely let his tongue wander nonchalantly in the moist valley around it, making sure however to return periodically to the central promontory. But, as she began responding, he took possession of her clitoris, sucking it deep into his mouth while kneading its crest with heavy strokes of his tongue. And then she began moaning and rocking her pelvis and he locked into her rhythm and danced with her a strange and magical dance in which the muscles of his neck, mouth and tongue moved as though innervated by Felicia's own nervous system, every movement of hers being instantly mirrored by him, so relentless had he been in the pursuit of her cunt. And then he progressively took control, becoming the choreographer as well as a dancer, enjoying his dual role as slave and tormentor, using his neck like a bull goring a matador until a shriek and a pulsation of her flesh informed him that she was climaxing.

Fearing that the spell might suddenly be broken, he immediately changed his position, unwinding his curled body and shoving his penis quickly into her vagina. He had proceeded to fuck her using short rapid strokes, not worrying about any refinements of technique, intent, rather upon catching up with Felicia who had already arrived at her destination. Momentarily, he climaxed also, and rolled next to her on the mattress, his left arm half encircling her body, his mouth breathing heavily against her cheek.

They laid there for a few minutes and he had a chance to look at her closely. The half-smile was gone now, and her facial expression was a mixture of serenity and sadness, as though the experience had stirred cherished memories or sowed a yearning for some improbable dream. Her eyes were moist, and perhaps he saw a tear hesitating at the edge of an eyelid.

They got up suddenly and dressed silently and he gave her the money, which she had neglected to demand in advance and had not mentioned since entering the house. She went to the bathroom first and then he followed. He was leaving, walking down the short hallway toward the front door of the apartment, when Felicia startled him by jumping at him from the doorway of the bedroom, her face aglow with a happy smile this time, and planted an enthusiastic kiss on his lips.

II

He is thinking of that kiss now. He has been thinking of that kiss often lately. At first he had not realized what a rare jewel it had been, that kiss. He had been too impressed with his own prowess in making a prostitute forget the necessary discipline of her trade to focus on any other aspect of that incident. Only later, when *decrepitudis moralis* had taught him more about the ways of whores, had he come to realize that, in the curiously inverted world of the prostitute, a kiss was the most extreme expression of sexual and personal intimacy, to be dispensed with a puritanical and virginal parsimoniousness. But now, he thinks of that magical kiss often. He can judge the currents of River by the frequency of its apparitions; and lately, River has taken him into some dark and depressing lagoons, and it has seemed almost as if River itself was winding down, giving up on him, refusing to furnish the energy to propel him toward any kind of meaningful place.

Place. That tenement in Boston, that had been a beautiful place, especially the coordinates of the point where his mouth had met with Felicia's wonderfully funky lower abdomen with its abscissas and ordinates of wrinkles and stretch marks. Who lives there now? What has happened there? It is nice and it is sad to think that somewhere in this universe there is a place, right now, that is being filled by loose, soft, deeply furrowed skin that is not being kissed and not being chewed.

How often she kisses him, Felicia. At night, when he is alone, drinking beer in the living room, she surprises him, darting from behind the couch, smiling that happy smile he had seen for only a second out of the forty or fifty minutes he had known her. Sometimes she kisses him while he is driving, jumping from behind the dark girders of the Brooklyn Bridge. He is grateful: it has become important, that kiss, since Lavonne left. Without it, certainly, the stench of the swamps where River has left him stranded would be unbearable.

III

Already, he feels embarrassed and he has not even touched her yet. He has been too busy, thinking of Felicia, and about River, and about Nerve. What the hell is her name? Her name... her name... Betty? Brenda? It starts with a B, that much he remembers. B...B...B... Beatrice! Yeah, that's it. Beatrice.

He has met her at Georgia's Peach, a singles' club. It hasn't been easy, getting himself there. Since Lavonne left, he has found himself alone, night after night, paralyzed, unable to fight River – which seemed bent upon immobilizing him – unable to find even a treacherous undertow, which, if it didn't kill him, might free him of the doldrums in which he has been floundering. He, horny Jerome, who could make a hooker forget she was a hooker; who could drive a woman to such paroxysms of passion that he felt embarrassed the next morning upon meeting the neighbors because he knew that the cries and moans had been audible in the adjacent apartments; who could plug into a woman's nervous system and drive her to passionate abandon with the very impulses of his horny soul; he, juicy Jerome, has been a virtual eunuch for almost six months. But tonight, this will change. Look out, River, I've started to swim. He has finally forced himself to go out and it has worked: now he is driving home and he has found a willing coconspirator, who is ready to aid and abet.

He is trying to think of something to say. They have hardly said a word since leaving the club and the silence is getting awkward. He should talk some shit; set the proper mood; give her that intense look that he has seen pimps use: the look with which a snake immobilizes a mouse. *I am man. You are woman. I fuck women. They love for me to fuck them. I move unhesitatingly and I grab what I want. I debase them and they beg for more. I use them and they don't complain. And then, I walk away and I don't give a shit. And they don't bother me, because they knew from the beginning what could be expected and what could not.*

"Did you see *One Flew Over the Cuckoo's Nest?*" The words have fallen out of his mouth and it's too late to stop them. They have just passed a theatre marquee and it suggested to him this way out of the awkwardness of their silence. But he knows it was a mistake. This is a serious motion picture that could easily lead to earnest conversation, and nothing could be more fatal to his plan.

What he really wants to do is to limit his involvement with her to one thing: sex. But that has always been difficult for him to do. He is almost as addicted to interesting conversation as he is to sex, and the excitement of engaging a stranger in a deep *tête-à-tête* almost matches the excitement of pussy hunting. He lacks the discipline of the pimp and of the expert seducer. But tonight, he will try.

Fortunately, she has not seen the movie. " I want to see it, but I didn't get around to it yet. I hear it's a good flick."

He lies and says, "Same here," and kills the conversation.

Should he take the Williamsburg Bridge or continue down the Bowery and take the Manhattan Bridge? Difficult decision. Always, difficult decisions. Best thing: wait till the last minute and let panic decide for you. At Delancy he makes a left turn: it will be the Williamsburg. He notices droplets on the windshield.

Rain. Good. Rain is sexy. The sky making love to Mother Earth, coming buckets, releasing all tension that has built up in the atmosphere. You can't see them but the clouds are up there – big scrotums floating in the air – and the wind strokes them and they ejaculate and their sperm falls all over Mother Earth, over her face, over her ass, all over.

"Hey, it's raining."

Brilliant deduction, bitch. "Yeah. You like rain?"

"Sometimes it's okay."

"Some rains are nice; some are a drag. Sometimes rain is sexy."

"I never thought of it that way," she says.

By that I mean it makes me feel sexy. Doesn't it make *you* feel sexy?"

"I guess so, a little bit, sometimes."

He is pleased with himself: now he is steering the conversation in the right direction. You got to talk shit to them. Talk some shit, baby. "You know, I have this fantasy sometimes: making it in the rain, somewhere in the country, under a tree. Maybe someday..."

"Don't look at me!"

"Oh no. I was only talking. Besides it's the wrong

time of year. You know, if this rain had fallen yesterday, it would have been snow."

"How's that?"

"Well, it was much colder yesterday."

"Oh."

Silence again. But not quite: the rain is getting heavier. He turns on the windshield wipers. Chik-a-chok, a-chik-a-chok, a-chik-a-chok. You can hear the counterpoint of the rain now impinging on the roof of the automobile and the cutting shush of wet tires on wet road. The white noise of the falling rain embraces him, shields him, isolates him. Beatrice is hardly there. He is a lonely astronaut and his ship is lost in space. Chik-a-chok, a-chik-a-chok, a-chik-a-chok.

He shakes his head. *Wake up, boy, you almost went through that red light.* He turns his head to the right and focuses on Beatrice. Funny, but he hasn't had a good look at her yet. The club was dark and he has not had a chance to see her in bright light. She looks passable, though. Not too big, not too small. Well, maybe just a little bit on the plump side. Not short, not tall. Her hair is light brown. Her face seems regular enough, but uninteresting. She doesn't seem to be wearing much makeup.

He tries to undress her mentally. Perhaps because he has drunk too much, it doesn't work. He doesn't feel the slight nervous twitch at the root of his scrotum that indicates that all systems are go; that there will be no trouble with erection; that the program will pass through the computer without a hitch; that performance will be flawless. He panics a little. *Jesus Christ, I shouldn't have drunk that much.*

"Don't you have a heater in this car?"

"Sure."

"Well, put it on, it's getting cold in here." Don't give me a hard time, bitch. Tonight, I'm the giver of hard times. "I'll put it on, but we're almost there."

"Good." She smiles brightly. "Don't mind me, I like to give people a hard time, sometimes."

First sign of life: a smile and a light-hearted quip. Well, maybe.

"How can you live in Brooklyn? How can anyone live in Brooklyn?" she says. "Aren't you scared to go out at night?"

"Didn't you say you live in the Bronx?" he replies.

"Yeah, good ole Bronx."

"And you talk about Brooklyn? How much of the Bronx is left, anyhow? I thought they were almost finished burning it down."

"That's the South Bronx you're talking about. Actually, there are many nice neighborhoods in the Bronx. Even some of the colored areas aren't all that bad."

Colored, she says. Very hip chick. "Yes, chalk one up for the Bronx: they got some good niggers there."

"I didn't say that."

"You're right; I shouldn't have said that. Well, I'll tell you what I think of the Bronx: some ten million years ago, Mars and Earth came dangerously close and the force of gravity of the Earth tore a chunk out of Mars, and that became the Bronx."

"So that makes me a Martian, hey?"

"Right."

"Would you kiss a Martian?"

"In the interest of good interplanetary relations, I might even go further than that."

He looks at her. She is staring straight ahead. She is not acknowledging his trial balloon. "Well, kiddo, we're here: my humble abode."

There's a parking spot right in front of the building. Good omen. *Higamus smiles upon me. Hogamus, you old motherfucker, you'll have to wait till tomorrow morning. Higamus time.*

IV

They are waiting for the elevator which seems stuck on the twelfth floor. He will use the time to prepare himself mentally: *tonight you think like a pimp, motherfucker*.

Only once had he done that really successfully for a whole evening: concentrated on pussy-pursuit and cock-over-pussy domination without deviating for one minute. And that had happened a long time ago, before *decripitudis moralis* had taken a firm hold. Surely, if he could do it then, he can do it now.

The phone rang and he answered.

"Hello."

"Hello, can I speak with Jerry."

"This is Jerry," he answered crossly, for he preferred being called Jerome.

"Jerry, why d'you sneak out last night? Made me look like a damn fool, leaving me all alone."

"What are you talking about? Who are you anyway?"

"Now aren't you the innocent one? You bastard. This is Joan. Who else you think it is, Lucille Ball?"

"Joan Haggarty?"

"No! Hey, you drunk? This is Joan." Joan something. (He had forgotten her last name almost as soon as they parted. He remembers Joan only because he originally thought it might be Joan Haggarty playing one of her silly jokes.)

"Hey, this is funny. I thought you were another Joan and you thought I was another Jerry."

"Shit!"

High-class broad, he remembers thinking. "My name is Jerome Dubinski and I don't know you, but we could fix that." He had bantered with her for a while, and then he had suggested a street comer where they could meet in an hour – "Can you be there in an hour? I'll be driving a blue Chevy with a banged-up right front fender" – and she had accepted. Quickly he changed, brushed his teeth, slapped a dash of cologne on his face and brushed his hair. How efficient he had been that night! He had gotten to the meeting place with minutes to spare. He was beginning to think she wouldn't show up when a slight girl wearing jeans and sneakers walked up to the car and said, “You Jerry?”

“You must be Joan. Hi.”

He took a second look at her and immediately the thought had crossed his mind that he had made a mistake: she was rather plain-looking and the blackheads on her forehead didn’t help. She could have used a little makeup but wasn’t wearing any. She was slim enough, but her body lacked any prominent features: no tits, no hips and no ass worth writing home about. Her jeans were somewhat dirty and he wondered how clean her pussy could be. She started walking to the other side of the car and he noticed that, although she wasn’t actually limping, there was something slightly amiss in her gait, as though something wasn’t quite right *up there*. But what had really bothered him was his strong suspicion that she had never finished grade school. Now, he had never been a snob – hated snobbery with a passion, in fact – but it had always seemed wrong and unfair to engage in sexual activity with someone with whom he could have no other possible bond of common interests. (He remembers Darryl and the gang, cruising in their late model convertibles, picking up women “of the working class;” taking them to a motel, a secluded parking spot, anywhere; getting them half drunk; fucking them; shoving their cocks into their mouths, and, as often as not, leaving them stranded and driving away none the worse for wear and, seemingly, unburdened by any feeling of guilt.)

He wanted to blurt out an excuse, forget the whole thing, and drive off, burning rubber. But then he had made his resolve: if it didn't bother Darryl and the others, why should it bother him? Tonight, he was going to concentrate: he was going to do nothing and say nothing but what would further his immediate interest, which was to get himself royally fucked, at any cost.

Joan was already sitting next to him in the car. He asked, "What's your poison?" she had replied "Gin," and he had said, "My family has a summer home just forty minutes from here, and it hasn't been used since August, so how about the two of us using it, I hate to see it go to waste," and she had answered, "Alright."

And so they drove off, stopping once for gin and once for mixers. She had dominated most of the conversation, being surprisingly fluent despite her obvious lack of education and her probably limited intelligence. What she said had not mattered much and he had not paid much attention until she mentioned having occasional epileptic fits.

Holy smoke, he thought, *I hope she doesn't have a fit tonight.* What if I don't pull out in time and I knock her up? The thought of a child – his child – shaking uncontrollably and frothing at the mouth was disquieting.

Again, he had second thoughts. But then he had remembered that he had stored a package of condoms under the spare tire, in the trunk. Everything was cool. Full speed ahead.

At the cottage, he made a log fire in the fireplace; then he mixed two strong drinks; and he sat on a polar-bearskin rug that was always stretched out on the floor, right in front of the grate, as though the bear was trying to warm its nose. He invited her to join him and she complied.

What ensued he remembers vaguely: in those days his fucking was primitive and simple. But one thing he remembers: he had not lost his concentration; he had not thought anything, said anything, or done anything to hinder in any way his pursuit of cunt or to diminish in any way the domination of cock over cunt. It had been a depressing triumph, but a triumph nonetheless, On the way back she said something about wanting to meet again and he answered with words that said nothing and made no commitments.

One more thing he remembers: a few months later, while hanging out downtown, he had seen her, walking toward him. Before she could spot him, he quickly crossed the street and got lost in the crowd. That experience left a bad taste in his mouth. Never before, nor ever after, had he felt this mixture of guilt and embarrassment.

V

The elevator has come, finally. They have ascended to the fifteenth floor. They enter his apartment and take their coats off. Although he intends to dim the lights later, he switches on a hundred-watt bulb because he wants to scrutinize her. He looks at her face. There is something indefinite about her features. They look no different under bright illumination than in the half-light of the club. Lips, nose, eyes, cheeks, blend into each other and, although there is nothing ugly about it, her face lacks character. Looking at it does not stir any hint of tremor in his genitals that the seismograph of his mind can detect. Quickly, he focuses on her body. Again, there is nothing wrong, but there are no points of interest. He searches for an intriguing curve of the breasts, a provocatively protruding hipbone, the sensuous promise of well-padded buttocks. Nothing. The seismograph registers nothing.

He inspects the room quickly. Has he removed every photo and memento of Lavonne and the boy?

It's not that he doesn't want Beatrice to see them; and not so much that he would resent answering questions; it's just that he is afraid of their effect upon him, and that it would feel almost sacrilegious to be messing – as Lavonne would say – with someone else, with her photo looking down from its spot on the wall and observing everything.

"Sorry there, vodka drinker, but I don't have any vodka. I do have gin, though, and scotch."

"D'you have any soda water?"

"Sure."

"I'll have a scotch and soda then."

"Comin' right up."

He disappears into the kitchen, mixes two strong drinks, and returns.

"Is it my imagination or is it cold in here" he says.

"It feels alright to me."

"Good. Why don't you look through my record collection and pick something you like."

She shuffles through the albums. "Don't you have anything good? All I see here is jazz."

"You must have missed the B Minor Mass. It's in there somewhere."

"Funny."

"Actually, I must admit to a strange perversion: I love jazz; I like classical; and I think rock sucks. I guess it's because I used to play the saxophone – still do, now and then."

"Different strokes for different folks," she shrugs. "Here, this looks passable."

She hands him an album of ballads by Nat King Cole.

Awkward. Every word he utters, every gesture he makes feels awkward and stiff. Even his thoughts are labored.

"Do you know that Nat King Cole was one of the best jazz pianists of his day, before he even thought of being a pop singer?"

"I didn't know that."

"Sure, I've heard that it was purely by accident than he became a singer. He was playing a gig in this club..."

"What's a gig?"

Jesus, where has she been? This broad is about

as hip as Whistler's Mother. "A gig means a job – a music job. Anyhow, he was playing in a club, fronting a trio, and the sidemen...

"Sidemen?"

"Yes – the drummer and the bass player – they didn't show up. They had an accident or something. So, Nat King Cole played by himself and, to make up for the missing bass and drums, he tried singing a few songs he knew the words to. Well, the patrons liked it so much that the next day the bass player and the drummer showed up, but the boss said, "Nat King Cole, either you sing or you shove that f-ing contract up yours," and that's how Nat King Cole became a singer.

I'd sing too, if you were going to shove a fucking contract up my ass," she says with just a hint of sarcasm.

Almost. Hearing her use the words *fucking* and *ass*, after he had chickened out with *f-ing* and *yours*, stirs an ever-so-slight tremor in that spot from which his testicles hang. He thinks of himself saying, *"Wouldn't you like something round and hard shoved up your fucking ass?"* but he knows that he would never have the nerve to say that so abruptly, so early in the game. And yet, what if he did say it? What could happen? Of course, she might look at him cross-eyed, grab her coat, and walk out the door. Big deal! And then, she might say, "Yes, that's what drives me up the wall, a big hard, slippery dick, fucking the shit out of my asshole." And he would jump at her and...

"Show business has done a lot for colored people," she adds, interrupting his train of thought.

"What's this *colored people* stuff? Hip people say *black people*, not *colored people*. And they're probably sick and tired of hearing how show business has been good to them."

"I guess I'm not very hip then."

He grunts. Gone. The slight erotic tremor has subsided. Again, words, movements and thoughts that had loosened momentarily become labored.

He will retreat to the bathroom, to the comfort of that toroidal security blanket, the toilet seat.

"Excuse me, honey, I'll be right back. Well, let me put this on for you first." He turns on the record player, places a disc on the turntable and adjusts the volume.

He locks the bathroom door. Although he feels no need to urinate or defecate, he unbuckles his belt, unzips his fly, lowers both trousers and underpants to the floor, and sits on the seat. He jumps up panic stricken. He did not notice that the toilet seat is in the vertical position and he is sitting on the hard porcelain, his buttocks stopping three inches lower than expected, the tip of his penis dipping into the cold water. Bad omen! Poor dick! Had come expecting to find temporary refuge in a warm pussy and, instead, ended up dunked in cold filthy water. Fucking Guardian Angel hounding him again. Well, not really: this time he can't blame it on GA. It's his responsibility to furnish an erection. All he can ask of GA is to not interfere. Not to create his usual impediments to sexual fulfillment: women who have – or claim to have – "the curse"; unexpected phone calls announcing sudden emergencies; the unexpected apparitions of mothers, brothers, old friends, old lovers, husbands, ex-husbands; sudden attacks of migraine; memory lapses about phone numbers, addresses, time; and the host of imaginative contingencies that Guardian Angel can conjure in his efforts to keep Jerome Dubinski pure despite his best intentions. *What damn business is it of yours, GA? Didn't I leave the Church ten years ago*? Perhaps the GA is the one link remaining with Mother Church. Mr. Big has told GA: "Stay on his case, GA. Keep frustrating him in every way, and don't forget his weakness. Perhaps frustration will bring him back to us." Yes, back to the fold, and then Guardian Angel would back off and he would be allowed all the pussy he wanted, almost guilt-free, provided he truly repent every few weeks or so and received absolution and, on occasion – having truly repented and received formal absolution – receive the unleavened bread under the gilded dome in the big stone building under the portals of which, upon leaving at the completion of the ritual, he might be lucky enough to meet yet another broad. *But what the hell am I raving about? GA tonight, it is* my *fiasco and unless you have some angelic trick up your sleeve I will not hold you responsible.*

He stands up and looks down at the offending toilet. For a moment he is tempted to try an old trick: occasionally, when a woman had invited him to her place, and he had a bladder full of urine ready for use, he had purposely aimed his piss right in the middle of the pond, instead of discreetly directing the stream at the side of the bowl, above the waterline, using the loud and offensive noise as a hunter's horn summoning the pack to the chase, announcing to his prospective quarry, "This is a real stud you got on your hands, baby, so brace yourself and abandon any thought of resistance and any hope for mercy." But tonight, he lacks the needed confidence. *Higamus, god of good times, you have deserted me.*

He lowers the seat. He sits. With his right hand he reaches down between his spread thighs, and he encircles his fingers around his flaccid penis. He knows he has drunk too much. He knows that since Bobo's death and the subsequent breaking down of his relationship with Lavonne, he has not been up to his usual game – definitely sub par. Still, perhaps a little self-stimulation would stir the sediments that seem to have settled in his testicles. All he wants is a little twitch – some slight assurance that an erection will be forthcoming.

Taking his penis between his thumb, and his index and middle fingers, he shakes it rapidly up and down.

Nothing!

He closes his entire hand around the shaft and slides it up and down, first slowly, then faster and faster.

Nothing!

Think pussy. Think tits: big hanging tits with long obscene nipples and big blue veins roadmapping the slick ivory skin.

Nothing!

Think pussy again: long-haired pussy; short-haired pussy; clean shaven pussy. A nice shiny, wide-open cunt. Think of full black-cherry-colored lips, pursed, ready to suck in your big hard cock.

Nothing!

He releases his penis and slouches forward, placing his elbows on his thighs. Ain't it a bitch how hard it is to live with Nerve? It's either too much or too little. He remembers how, during his high school years, Nerve would start working on him, just as spring was approaching, destabilizing him progressively; how he just knew he was going to do something stupid – any day now – and get in trouble with school or with his parents. And sure enough, it would happen. And he would have to suffer the consequences, but at least Nerve would quiet down and leave him alone for a while. It's always too much or too little. You can't win. When Nerve quiets down, at first you're happy, you're cool, you're in control, you can relax. But then, just let Nerve fall asleep in his hole, somewhere deep in your flesh; just let him play hooky for a few days – for a week or so – and you start wondering. What's wrong with me? I'm loosing it! Must be getting old! Can't kick ass anymore, not even my own – the one that really needs a swift kick. Can't hardly get it up! You can't win. Since Lavonne left, Nerve has been in a slump.

Usually, when River became too turgid, he could count on Nerve to kick his butt and make him swim out of the swamps and eddies, and find, again, the mainstream; the swift white water; the dangerous, bruising but exhilarating rapids and cataracts. If all else failed, he could mentally make River antigravitate – it could do that, yes – and he would feel himself floating and flowing along a rollercoaster River, passing through, over, and around fluffy silver-lined clouds, and he would get almost high on the motion, on the freedom and abandon of it, and on the feeling that he could make it go on and on as long as he wanted it to go on like that.

But now even this magical trick is failing him. There will be no levitation tonight, neither of River nor of that moribund and cumbersome appendage hanging uselessly between his thighs.

He turns to flush the toilet (there is no need, but he is embarrassed to spend so much time in the bathroom without some justification) and he suddenly bursts into a half-muffled guffaw, which he immediately camouflages by coughing and clearing his throat. Under the toilet tank he has discerned a grayish box of facial tissues that had fallen from its perch on the tank cover, and it reminds him of a Polaroid camera of the same color hidden some years ago in a similar location.

Wendy, the supertease, with whom he had not communicated in months had called him. "I need some nude shots and you're the only person I can trust for this." Fine. Was that a compliment or an insult? "The only person I can trust!" What she probably meant was, "the only whimp I can trust." Still, *noblesse oblige*, so he had taken his old Polaroid, and, stopping first to buy some black and white film and some flash bulbs, he had driven to her place, all the while wondering why, after all this time, out of the blue, Wendy would make this strange request. But then, you could expect almost anything from a woman who was into esoterica, ran her life according to the ouija board, and had regular conversations with her dead grandfather. She probably wanted to answer – on a whim – some personal ad in a swingers' magazine that had included a request for "a revealing photo and a self-addressed stamped envelope." Lots o'luck Mr. Advertiser (or Ms. – he had always suspected that Wendy was bisexual). Or Mr. and Ms., or Mr. and Mr., or any combination of any number of either. He, she, or they would learn that, with Wendy, there was a wide gulf between implied promise and actual delivery.

She greeted him at the door wearing a drab unglamorous bathrobe. After the usual cup of herbal tea – one of her many rituals – she simply let the bathrobe slip off her shoulders, and said, almost casually, "Well, let's get on with it." She immediately flopped on the bed, which consisted of a mattress lying on the floor with neither frame nor box spring, and adopted a most provocative pose, her legs spread wide, her crotch thrust forward, her hands separating the pubic hair and exposing the moist pinkness of her vagina. He could have thrown a rock with his penis, so instantaneous and violent had been his erection. (Certainly, she had noticed the bulge in his pants, but she made no comment or other acknowledgement.)

Damn, damn, damn! How he wanted to dive into her and ravish her right there and then! How his tongue craved to taste the musty sweetness of her wide-open cunt! How his cock pleaded to be released from the binding of his pants and left free to burrow into her exposed flesh!

But he knew her too well: she would parry his thrust and with a voice barely tinged with alarm, would chide him: "Now, come on, Jerome, control yourself, just think of me as a model." And, of course, she would end with the *pièce de résistance*: "I thought I could trust you." And, indeed, hadn't she said on the phone: "You're the only person I can trust with this."? And, of course, always the gentleman, he would back off, would not force himself upon her, even though he could hardly be blamed for doing so.

So it was better, he concluded, not to do it – at least not right now.

"Well, go on, take a picture," she said.

"Take your time," he replied. I haven't even put the film in the camera. I'll be ready in a flash – dig it? –

flash."

A few minutes later, he started taking photos, each more outrageously lascivious than the previous one. Willingly, she exposed all the orifices of her body – vagina, anus, mouth – even, in one shot, stretching one of her breasts until she could clasp her teeth on the nipple. For another pose, she vigorously massaged her clitoris until it stood out like a red button on a pink shirt and her pussy lips glistened with the pungent juice of her aroused genitalia.

All the while he progressively divested himself of his clothes until wearing nothing but shorts and socks, and she had said nothing, as though not noticing. With each shot he would remove a garment while the chemicals developed the picture, then he would peel off the photo from the negative, stacking the former on the thickening pile – after showing it to her – and dropping the latter on the floor.

Suddenly she asked, "How many exposures you got left?"

"Just one," he answered.

"Good thing I asked, I want one bondage shot."

"What? " he exclaimed, incredulously.

"Tie me up for the last shot."

He couldn't believe it. Wendy would never put herself in such a vulnerable position. Not Wendy! But she had said it. Must have flipped her wig! "What with? D'you have any rope?" "Look in the closet, there's some scarves."

He found two long silk or nylon scarves. Bending her legs at the knees and pulling her thighs up toward her chest, he tied her wrists to her ankles, right to right and left to left, passing the arms inside the thighs and across to the outside of her lower leg, as though braiding her limbs. This way, it was impossible for her to bring her thighs together to close off her crotch. Meanwhile, he made his resolve. How much can a guy take? Certainly she wanted it. Wanted him to take advantage of her vulnerability, to ravish her while she was helpless.

He was already kneeling. He had placed his body between her legs and was holding his penis in one hand and reaching with the other toward her vagina when the doorbell rang.

"Wha...?"

Both froze in panic.

"Don't answer the door: nobody home," he said,

a fraction of a second before realizing that the lights were on and the hi-fl was blaring.

Again the doorbell rang.

"Wendy, this is Mom and Carmen." The voice seemed to fill the room.

"Oh shit, my mother and sister. What are these fuckin' people doing here now?" Wendy whispered, adding: "Sh... they can hear when they push the *listen* button.

Again the intercom blared: "Come on Wendy, let me in. I don't feel like emptying my handbag to find the damn key."

"That's right, I gave her a key last week," whispered Wendy.

Unfreezing, Jerome sprung into frenzied action, gathering his clothes with swift swipes of his arms, snatching the camera, and grabbing the photos. Dodging furniture and jumping over a wastepaper basket, he was headed for the bathroom when a distressed and anxious voice said: "Untie me, you fool!"

Oh shit! Wendy was still trussed like a bird in the oven. He flung everything into the bathroom and ran, dodged and jumped his way back to her. He managed to release her quickly, and in a flash made it back to the bathroom. Not stopping to turn on the light or close the door, he picked the photos out of the pile of clothes and threw them in the hamper. Hearing the click of the latch, he closed and locked the bathroom door. He then groped for the light switch until he remembered that it was on the outside.

Oh great! Perfect day, so far. One for you, Guardian Angel! In pitch darkness he dressed. He hid the camera behind the toilet, under the tank, at a similar spot to where the tissue box was lying.

(He interrupts his reminiscence long enough to pick up the box and place it back on the tank cover, then he returns to his musing.)

He flushed the toilet, and, consciously etching a smile, he boldly opened the door and stepped out. Wendy, wearing her bathrobe, was sitting on the mattress, facing her mother and sister who were each sitting in a chair, and... oh no! ... between them, lying on the floor, were the negatives, some of them face up, and – damn! – the negative images were quite clearly discernable. His mouth dropped slightly, his breathing stopped, and his ears tingled as he blushed. How he wished he could melt at will and pour himself through the cracks between the boards! Everyone was looking anywhere but down and everyone was acting as if no one had noticed anything, but everyone knew that everyone knew that everyone knew. *Guardian Angel, I never knew you had such a devilish sense of humor.*

He regained his composure, and Wendy, ever the unflappable one, introduced him to her kin. To save face – whatever was left to save – he joined the conversation that had started and even bravely said a few witty things. Then, under the pretext that he had to rise early in the morning, he excused himself and left.

Once in his car, he exploded in a screaming voice: "Ah shit! – ...double shit! ...fuck! ...triple fuckin' fuck! Of all the stupid shit-eating cock-sucking, mother-fucking luck!!" All the way home he kept up a barrage of such curses, without uttering or thinking a single coherent sentence. And, to make matters worse, he had left the dirty pictures in the hamper, and he knew that Wendy would never surrender even one of them. Shitfucksuck...!

It's funny now, but it wasn't funny then. Jerome stands up, turns, and this time he completes his intended actions: he flushes the toilet, washes his hands, and leaves the room.

VI

"My turn," she says. She has helped herself to another scotch and soda and she takes it to the bathroom. Fine; he wants to be alone for a while. Take your time. He reaches for the bottle, but snaps his arm back. Enough is enough is enough.

He has only one framed picture of Lavonne and he has hidden it under the couch. As he crosses the room he glances for a moment at the effigy of Higamus, standing guard, eye-level on the third shelf, next to the *History of Western Philosophy*. He retrieves the photo from its hiding place.

It has been six long months since he was last with her, but here she is smiling at him from behind the glass cover. It was that beautiful face that attracted his attention that day in Bibleway Church: a face molded out of pure terra cotta, fired but unglazed, the monochromaticism of its features – full, as should be expected, yet finely chiseled – projecting a classical and mythical quality, as though inspired by a clay statuette from an ancient Ethiopian tomb.

Ashes to ashes and dust to dust. Had he not met her at a funeral, and was it not a funeral that had marked the beginning of the end of their relationship?

It was at the funeral of Harold Johnson's mother that he first saw her. It had been an initiation of sorts: his first time inside a sanctified church. Hand clapping, preaching, tambourine shaking, swaying, all had intrigued him, but it was the parade for the last viewing of the corpse that really startled him. The family filed one by one before the open casket. The men were stoic enough, but every woman carried on as though auditioning for some Hollywood Technicolor funeral: sobbing, screaming, shaking, writhing – a few had even fainted – as she confronted the waxy mask in the coffin. Only Lavonne did not lose her composure; that's what made him notice her. *Wow, he thought, what a striking face!* It would have been inappropriate indeed for such a strong and proud face to be seen hollering and putting on airs.

Throughout the remainder of the service, and again at the cemetery, he kept glancing in her direction, as though mesmerized by the magnetism of her features.

Only at the subsequent reception for family and close friends did she adopt, in his eyes, a more realistic flesh-and-blood dimension.

"You must be a member of the family," he said.

"Almost. Betty Johnson was my godmother. We were very tight."

"I'm a good friend of Harold. We work together for Social Service."

Seeing her at close range, he perceived a sensuous quality to the movements of her lips. He had not noticed that in church, nor the passionate and primitive salience of her cheekbones.

"You'll have to excuse me," she said. "I have to pick up my son next door."

"For some reason, I thought you were single."

"I am," she smiled.

She returned in a few minutes, carrying a toddler in her arms.

"Meet Bobby," she said, "better known as Bobo."

"Hi Bobo. I'm Jerome Dubinski. Hey, say, who's that beautiful lady you're with."

"My name is Lavonne, Jerome. Lavonne

Campbell."

"Pleased to meet you. How old is Bobo?"

"Bobo is two and a half."

"He's a very handsome young man.

"I think so, too, and I'm very proud of him."

There was something in the way she held the boy that had pleased him. As he looked at her cradling her son tenderly and sensuously in her arms, he had actually felt the beginning of an erection straining against the Dacron polyester of his shorts.

And why not? Why only from tits and asses, sensuous mouths and swaying hips and such? Why not get a hard-on because you perceive kindness or a keen intelligence or a delightful sense of humor? Men are so stupid about these things! Of course, you can't suck on a fine sense of humor, and you can't pat a keen intelligence, and you can't fondle a deep concern for the underprivileged.

Regardless! Here was a woman who made him horny, not because of her tits or her ass, but because of the way she touched and held her son and because of the picture of maternal solicitude she projected. Fascinating woman!

With mock seriousness, he shook Bobo's hand. "I hope I can get to know you better."

"Oh, Bobo's very friendly. Never rejects the open hand of friendship."

"Perhaps I could drop him off at his place, on my way home."

"He can't leave right now, because his mother promised to help clean up."

"I can wait."

"Good. And now let me go do some work. Oh, by the way, did you try the meatballs? I made them. The brown sauce is my secret."

"Delicious! Say, why don't you leave Bobo with me? I think we'll get along."

"You like babies? Most men don't know what to do with them. You know, I'm beginning to like you." She left the child with him. He sat Bobo face-to-face astride his knees, holding him firmly by the hands.

"Hi, Bobo."

"Bobo, Bobo," the kid replied.

"You have a nice mama.

"Lavonne."

"Yes, Lavonne."

"Bobo, good Bobo."

"Sometimes, I'm sure, bad Bobo."

"Bad Bobo. Lavonne?"

"Hey kid! I want to see your smile."

He pinched the boy's jowl lightly. Bobo beamed and Jerome noticed how dazzlingly white his teeth looked against the dark background of his face.

Handsome kid. Darker skinned than his mother. Had the same wide, boldly arched nose, though. Hair was thinner than Lavonne's and the whites of his eyes – like his teeth – stood in sharply limpid contrast to the dark hue of his face. Happy eyes. Happy, easy smile. Something about the symmetric ovals of those eyes reminded him of Lavonne. In one respect, the two of them were very dissimilar: whereas Lavonne's features displayed a marked uniformity of color, Bobo's were a study in vivid contrasts.

It had always been his practice to kiss little girls, but to shake hands with little boys. Bobo, though, looked so kissable with those fat cheeks and that warm smile that, pulling him gently by the hands, he brought the cherubic face close to his and deposited a fat and noisy kiss on its cheek.

When Lavonne had finished her work, they climbed into his station wagon and, in barely ten minutes, arrived at her place on Rogers Avenue. She was carrying a shopping bag full of leftover sandwiches and soda pop cans, as well as the baby and a shoulder bag full of diapers, milk bottles, and other such accessories. He helped her carry all this to her apartment and she asked him in.

It was a small three-room apartment. They sat in the living room, which was dominated by a crucifix above the doorway to the bedroom and a picture of Christ on the opposite wall. "I think you're more religious than I am"' he said. "In fact, I don't bother with religion at all."

"I forgive you. Now you only have to worry about Him. Can I bring you a glass of Coke or ginger ale. I'm sorry. I don't have any liquor or beer here. My church don't believe in drinking."

"Nothing. Thank you." He had always had trouble with women who didn't drink. Once, he remembers vividly and painfully, it had been his misfortune to be invited into the apartment of a woman he met at a dance, who didn't drink, and who, it soon became apparent, did not like to kiss. Although she had obviously been anxious for carnal adventure, he left in disgust, not even bothering to find an excuse, because, deprived of his usual props and denied his familiar rituals he had been unable to decide on his next move. What the hell do you do with a woman who won't drink and doesn't kiss?

"Does Bobo get to see his father often?"

"Very rarely, and that's fine with me. His father isn't really interested. I guess you can say I made a mistake." She shrugged and smiled. "In a way, I made a mistake. But in a way, I'm glad. Now, I couldn't think of being without Bobo. When I told that bastard I was pregnant, all he could say was 'Get an abortion. Get an abortion. Ain't nothing to it. Get an abortion.' And he was a churchgoer too. Kept talking 'bout how he was saved. Look at that kid: Would you take a knife and cut him up? Flush him down the drain? Like nothing had happened? That ain't right, no way. That's a living person you got in there."

"That's one reason I don't bother with religion anymore." Jerome interjected. "Too many hypocrites."

"Well, that turned me off too. But then I'm in the choir over there and I love good gospel music. So I stay in. Look, I'm no philosopher: I'm just a simple little black girl. When I go to Bibleway Church and I sing and I shake that tambourine, I feel good. It's one long all-year party over there. Shoot, we party more than the sinners do. But no alcohol and no smoking. You know, I wasn't always saved. I used to drink... and worse."

"Look, Lavonne. I, ah, I think I like you... a lot. That's funny, you know, because I always avoided church-type women. You know, I was raised Catholic and I always figured, you know, if a chick – I mean, a woman – was too much into the church thing, well, she just wouldn't be interested in the things I like and the way I like to live, you know." He hated this: every time he had to force himself to say something that was difficult and embarrassing to say, but had to be said, he kept repeating that dumb phrase, *you know*, over and over like a broken record.

Lavonne looked at him earnestly. "What you're trying to tell me is that those religious Catholic chicks don't screw. And you're saying this because you're trying to find out where I'm at. Right?"

Damn! There was one forthright woman.

"Well, only because I like you and it's difficult because I don't know how to approach you. We're not at a party and you don't drink. And you have a baby with you. So, I can't put some romantic music on and say, 'Would you like to dance?' And I don't want to do something and you say to yourself, you know, 'All those white guys are the same.'"

"I understand. But it's not so easy for us either. You want me to let you know where I'm at, but I don't want to say anything that'll make you say, 'All those black chicks are the same.' Do you always expect a white girl to let you know where she's at when you've only known her a few hours?"

He decided then that he should trust his instincts and not worry about where she was at, and he knew that, if his instincts were tuned in, he was going to fall in love, whatever the hell that means, with Lavonne – and with Bobo, who, in his mind, seemed to be an inseparable part of her.

He just looked at her with a half-smile and nodded. "Okay... Alright... I understand. I'm sorry if I came on too strong. It's because I'm not very good at certain kinds of games – the kind of games that men and women get trapped into playing – and I can feel a strong vibration between you and me and I don't want to mess it up just because I can't play the usual games... Shit, I can walk up to a puppy dog on the street and say, 'Hey fellow, come over here. I want to play with you,' and that puppy'll come and put his two front paws on my legs and wag his tail; and I can walk up to Bobo and say, 'Hey kid, how you doin'?' and he'll smile at me; but I can't do it with a woman, even if I get that kind of feeling from her... and why not? I wish I could understand why not."

"Why should it be so easy?" Lavonne said. "Why should anything worthwhile be so easy? Do I have to be easy, just to prove to you I don't play games?"

He felt then that he had broken through the defensive shell that women and men so often build as protection against each other and he felt strong, confident and exhilarated.

"Lavonne, can I touch you?"

"Of course, I'm not made of gold."

"Can I kiss you?"

"I guess so," she said, somewhat hesitatingly. She had dropped her arms at her side and had looked at him with an expression he couldn't quite fathom. He took her left hand in his right hand and he brought his left hand up until it lightly touched her chin and then he turned her head to his right and carefully deposited the gentlest of kisses on her left cheek.

"I have to leave now."

Not true: he had nothing to do. He was afraid that, were he to stay any longer, he might say or do something that would break the magic. He had broken enough barriers for one day: he couldn't stand it any longer.

"Lavonne, would you like to see me again?"

"Jerome, I wouldn't have asked you in if I didn't think you were someone I would want to see again."

He picked up Bobo and kissed him and was walking out when Lavonne stepped in front of him and kissed him, just like Felicia had kissed him in that little apartment near Massachusetts Avenue in Boston, so many twists and turns of River ago.

He saw her again the next day, and on the next day after that, and then they made love, and then they had decided to try living together in his place, which was somewhat larger and better furnished than hers.

VII

DOO-dee-doo, DOO-dee-da,
DOO-dee-doo-dee-dum-dee-da.

He is humming a silly little ditty he had composed to fit the words of a doggered he had read somewhere:

Higamus, Hogamus
Woman is monogamous;
Hogamus, higamus
Man is polygamus.

He tries to remember who it was attributed to. Was it Benjamin Franklin? Anyhow, the legend is that the great man was awakened one night from a dream in which had been disclosed to him the ultimate secret of the universe. He wrote down the revelation on a sheet of paper that was lying on his desk. Upon rising in the morning he rushed to the desk, aglow with anticipation, only to read this silly poem.

Still, there's a grain of truth in it, DOO-dee-doo, DOO-dee-da. Catchy phrase, higamus-hogamus, higamus-hogamus.

One day Jerome had been holding an Eskimo soapstone statuette of a winged creature, half man, half bird, absentmindedly tossing it from hand to hand, when he suddenly decided – for no reason – that the icon should have a name, and that Hogamus was a perfectly fine name for it. On second thought, he imagined that Hogamus was rather the name of some mystic entity of which the statuette was but a symbol. But then, who – or what – was Hogamus? A deity yes, that's it, a god. The great and powerful god Hogamus. But what about Higamus? Can't have a Hogamus without a Higamus, DOO-dee-doo, Doo-dee-da. Higamus and Hogamus had to be brothers – yes, twins. Twin gods.

Looking at the stern eagle-like face of the statuette, Jerome had decided that Higamus was the god of stern things: hard work, responsibility, punctuality, frugality, and savings accounts at banks covered by Federal Deposit Insurance. Which left the fun job for his brother, the god of good times, booze, sex, wild parties, dirty jokes and overdrawn checking accounts – at banks covered by Federal Deposit Insurance.

But a god must have an effigy; and he had none for Higamus. Glancing across the room, his eyes stopped at a porcelain figurine of a plump, jowly and jolly man with a balding pate and a nice round tummy. But something was lacking: a mythic quality of some sort; a mystical *je ne sais quoi*. But then a brilliant idea popped in his brain – a stroke of genius, no less. Walking over to the artifact, he placed it in front of a desk lamp in such a way that a clear shadow was projected on a nearby wall. Yes, the shadow, not the figurine, would represent Higamus. Quite fittingly, then, Higamus would be a night god, and his twin a day god – an efficient scheme for celestial shift-work (although overtime was necessary, as when one wanted to fuck in the afternoon, or had to bring work home from the office).

How well he had slept that night, Jerome, secure in the knowledge that two deities were watching over him. It was only a few weeks later that it had dawned upon him that there was little you could do with two gods if you didn't have a religion to go along with them. And so, in another flash of warped insight was born the religion of H'gamism (pronounced Huh-ga-mism).

Instantly, Jerome had decreed that H'ganism also had at least two minor deities – angels, of sorts – in River and Nerve.

After the initial flush of excitement, he suddenly sank into a mini depression. How could such a small itty-bitty religion compete with the giants of the industry: Christianity, Islam, Hinduism, and all the others? But just as quickly a smile returned to his countenance: he had every reason to feel proud of being a H'gamist, for here is a rare thing indeed, a clean religion – a religion that has never mounted a crusade against another faith; that has never conquered lands and imposed itself with the cutting edge of the scimitar; that has not used its priests as the advance guard for the rape and exploitation of another culture; that has not been used to keep women, slaves, and the destitute in their place; that has never tortured a single heretic or burned a single crazed old hag at the pyre; and that has not wrested one penny from the poor and gullible for the support of its clergy. Yes, a H'gamist and proud of it of it!

But the best thing about H'gamism – and in this it out-zens Zen itself – is that its most important tenet is to not take itself too seriously. Higamus and Hogamus are gods in the same sense that Bugs Bunny is a rabbit; and H'gamism is a religion in the same sense that the School of Hard Knocks is a school. Of course, the same thing can be said of most – perhaps all – other gods and religions. The difference is that H'gamism realizes this and accepts this. No need to get into a barroom brawl over it. All you have to do is say: "Hey man, I was only kidding. It's just for fun." A disposable religion. Of course, all religions are, to some extent, disposable, depending on the degree of integrity of the disposer; but in H'gamism you have disposability without hypocrisy. A perfect religion.

And, oh yes, one more thing: H'gamism is not a proselytizing religion. In fact it only exists in the mind of one individual, Jerome Dubinsky: prophet, pope and parishioner. Even Lavonne – from whom, during most of their relationship, he had kept almost no secrets had never been told. Heck, she thought he was a little crazy to start with, so why push it, hey? H'gamism, the perfect religion.

Doo-dee-doo, DOO-dee-da.
DOO-dee-dum-dee-da.

VIII

Jerome walks over to a corner of the room where a tenor saxophone is leaning against the wall. He picks up the instrument and wets the reed. The last track on the Nat King Cole album is ending. Jerome puts the instrument to his mouth and plays a counterline against the last few phrases. The turntable clicks off automatically but he keeps on playing. He is trying to get on his tenor a sweet and sexy sound like Johnny Hodges gets on alto. He will seduce her with his music. The syrupy notes ooze out and infiltrate the bathroom. Sweet, sexy, silk-and-satin bedroom music. Pussy-tickling music. An ode to vaginal secretions.

The bathroom door opens and a river of light floods his space as Beatrice approaches.

"Hey, you sound real good, like a professional."

He stops and lowers the instrument. "Well at one point I did think of turning pro, of *dedicating my life to jazz*," says he in a sarcastically bombastic tone. "But then something happened: I didn't."

"What happened to change your plans?"

"Nothing happened. What happened is that I didn't become a professional musician, that's all. That was one of the important non-events of my life. No reason. I coulda made it. At least I coulda tried. I didn't," he adds with a shrug of his shoulders.

"You're strange." She shakes her head and smiles at him.

"We're all strange." He winks at her.

"Play some more."

He intones a few random notes, trying to think of a tune, but a sharp angry knock from an adjacent apartment reminds him that it's after midnight.

"Concert's over. No encores."

"You mind mixing me another drink? But only put half a shot in it, okay? I gotta go to work tomorrow."

He lowers the volume, turns the record over, then goes to the kitchen to fix her a weak drink. He decides, again, not to have any more. When he returns, she is standing in front of the bookcase, looking the books over. He hands her the drink and flops into an overstuffed chair. Will she sit in his lap or choose the sofa across the room? She takes the sofa. Good. He is not ready. The game has been postponed, but *only* postponed, my dear. There is silence between them again, but it is not a particularly awkward silence. Lavonne's picture is under the couch, just where Beatrice is sitting. He can feel his mouth stretch into a half smile. She doesn't seem to notice. He stands for an instant and arranges the figurine and the desk lamp. He turns on the latter and turns off the main light. Fortunately he had screwed in a dim red bulb before leaving for the club. "That's better," she says. He returns to the chair. Higamus, the shadow god, is clearly delineated on the wall, completely surrounding Beatrice. How fitting. Not just a coincidence, no sir. It is so dark there that she almost looks like a black woman. He tries to see her as Lavonne, to see Lavonne in her,. to meld both into one entity. Why? Don't know. Since she doesn't turn him on, he is perhaps trying to fool himself into an aroused state. It would be the first time: strange, but in the six months since the separation, he has not used Lavonne's photo, nor his mental image of her, nor the recollection of any of their many memorable erotic episodes to feed his masturbatory fantasies, And, God knows, Jerome Dubinski has jerked off. How else would six months of celibacy be possible? Rather, he has used pornographic magazines, old memories of other girl friends, and vivid scenarios of which some woman he had seen that day – sometimes even a co-worker or a client was the star.

He digresses for a moment. He is thinking of Jackie, a client that he had found so sexually enticing that he had been tempted to break his code of ethics – both professional and personal – and make at least an attempt at her seduction. On the day of their first interview, he had been so aroused that, upon arriving home from work, he had hurried to his bed and, quickly divesting himself of his pants and shorts, made wild, freaky, fierce, superhuman sex with her phantasm. Oh! How she had screamed for more, inside his brain! How she had willingly – even enthusiastically – acquiesced to his every wish, every demand! How she had allowed him to place her in all kinds of outlandish positions! And then, the indescribable release, the sweet explosion, and, for a moment, the annihilation of everything in the universe except for that fantastic sensation. And then, of course, Jackie had unobtrusively faded into near-oblivion, only to return later in the evening, and again upon his waking in the morning. And everyday for almost a week her ghost had returned, but each time with less vividness and less insistence. Exorcism by ejaculation. It works. Won't get you accepted into the St. Theresa of Avila chapter of the Virgins' and Martyrs' Club; but it works. Better than losing your job, and, more importantly, better than breaking your code. Poor Miss Jackie! Never knew what he had stolen from her, nor how shamefully he had used her. And she was none the worse for it either. The perfect crime!

On their second interview, although Jackie looked just as sexy and beautiful as before – more so, in fact, since she showed a fair amount of cleavage – and although her demeanor had been friendly to the point of inviting some kind of advance on his part, his conduct had been thoroughly professional and ethical: the exorcism had worked.

But back to Beatrice-as-Lavonne: Jerome tries to focus his mind and unfocus his eyes so as to see her sitting there, within the shadow space of Higamus. Gradually, Lavonne invades the features of Jerome's perception of Beatrice. Finally, the transformation is complete and it is Lavonne that is sitting there; not the brokenhearted Lavonne of after Bobo's death; not the Lavonne he doesn't know anymore, living somewhere in another city doing God knows what; but the Lavonne of before the heartbreak, the Lavonne that had been with him inside even when she wasn't physically present, and that had the magical power to make everything he did meaningful and fun.

How pretty she looks. Yet he know that she is only a ghost; that if he started walking toward her, she would fade gradually, and, at the moment of their touching, she would vanish, and it would be Beatrice that would be sitting there. So he too will become a ghost. He will send his specter to meld with hers. He approaches her slowly as if trying to surprise her. He performs what had become almost a ritual, the sequence of movements of their very first kiss, something he often did to initiate sexual play with her. Again, the gentle placing of his left hand under her chin; the slow pivoting of her head until her left cheek is at the right angle; the lowering of his head, as if drawn by a magnet; the soft cushioned impact of his lips on her satiny skin. But then, with tender ferocity, both their mouths open and converge, and their tongues intertwine in a frenzied *pas-de-deux*, both of them trying to suck the other's buccal flesh into his own, neither noticing the grinding clash of teeth against teeth. One hand clamps a breast, the fingers locating through her clothing the prominent and habitually erect nipple, and rolling it forcefully between thumb and forefinger. The other hand reaches for her crotch and rubs its bony promontory in time with the back and forth rolling of her nipples. And then, with the quickness of a summer squall's evanescence, the scenario changes and the ghost of Lavonne is lying on the couch and Jerome's shadow self is protectively arched over her, all of his body in intimate contact with hers, but lightly, most of its weight being supported by his elbows and knees. And he is saying beautifully simple things like, "Lavonne I love you so much," or silly things like "Moma, popa's gonna do you good," and she is thrilling him by repeating his name softly, "Jerome... oh Jerome... my Jerome... Jerome, baby!"

That's the way it had been, their lovemaking: almost without foreplay, not because they were brutish and crude, but because they were both strongly sexual, and because they had complete physical and emotional understanding of each other. And it had been just as tender when it seemed almost violent as it was intense when it seemed gentle. Boy, how that woman could claw his back! Sometimes, in the morning, they would see red lines on the sheet, where the scratches had bled. And sometimes, after a wild session, she would have one or two light bruises and neither would have any idea how or when, and they would both laugh.

But if they usually skipped foreplay, they more than compensated in afterplay. That's what he remembers most fondly: those long sweet minutes after lovemaking, when they would both bask in the afterglow of their fucking, and he would do things like stroke her nape, or trace "I love you" on her back with his finger, or play with her hair (how he loved the brush-like feel of her afro); and she would blow in his ear, or do baby things like tweaking his nose and pinching his cheek, or she would disappear under the top sheet and fold her body until her mouth touched his limp, wet penis, and she would suck it in just to show him how she loved it – and loved him – and maybe the whole scene would start again.

Funny, but no matter how far out and wild their lovemaking could get, nothing they did together ever felt dirty or sick. His body could make love to her or fuck her, but his mind always and only made love. He remembers one time: in the middle of some furious hard-driving sex, he suddenly imagined a Peeping Tom peering through the window between the incompletely closed curtains; and he had imagined this coarse, perverted soul thinking, "Wow, this boy's fuckin' the shit outa that bitch;" and the thought had come to Jerome, in the middle of his frenzied gyrations, that such a person could never understand the essence of the act he was unlawfully ogling, because that essence was in the mind of the lovers, not in their movements, not in their sweat, not in their cries. The same curve of lips and drawing of facial muscles can be a smile or a smirk: it's all the mind of the smilers. And it's all in the mind of the fuckers.

Only once, during the good times, did he have any second thoughts about the absolute cleanliness and propriety of their relation. While making love to Lavonne, he had heard Bobo cough and he had suddenly realized that just knowing that Bobo was sleeping like a little angel in the next room added something to his lovemaking: made it deeper and more meaningful. And he had lost his erection because he had started wondering if perhaps there was not something a little bit unhealthy about this, since, in a sense, the child was a passive participant in the act. But then he had quickly dismissed that feeling: was there not a perfectly natural and logical connection between sex and children? And had he not, from the beginning, accepted child and mother as one entity? This mental trip however was one of the few he had deliberately not shared with Lavonne.

It was only after Bobo's death that he entertained second thoughts about the relationship. And these, of course, had gotten more insistent after the separation.

For one thing, he had not been quite as colorblind as he had believed. Thinking back, it did seem that the color difference had added excitement and exoticism. Jerome had found a certain satisfaction in the contrast of her dark brown skin against his much lighter complexion. But there was no harm in that. At times, however, he had been more critical of himself, as though looking for guilt, perhaps hoping to find – in the guilt – a partial explanation for the collapse of their love. Would he have made the same effort at meeting her had she been white? Had he not been playing the role of iconoclast and rebel, rejoicing in the shock value of his miscegenation? And his love for Bobo? Could it be that it wasn't quite real? That he had merely been playing father? Playing white-liberal-flower-child-hipster-beat-generation father? But then, if you insist on being Freudian to the nth degree, doesn't everyone get diagnosed as sick? Jerome had come to the conclusion that his conscience was clear, and that his love had been healthy and pure.

One night, though, driving up Eighth Avenue in Manhattan, watching the parade of whores, pimps – most of whom were black – and Johns – most of whom were white – he reflected on how prostitution was a slave occupation, and on how the pimps were in the business of keeping their own people in bondage. And this had prompted another self-examination. Had he unconsciously seen, in Lavonne, the black whore? Had he done that just a little bit? Had he fallen for some stereotype such as "all black women are hot and sexy"? Was there anything of the master-slave syndrome in his relationship with Lavonne?

Once, while Bobo was sound asleep, he passed by the open bathroom and saw Lavonne sitting on the toilet, urinating. He stopped and stood there, just looking. "Why you looking at me funny like that?" she said while reaching for the doorknob. He blocked the door's path with his foot. She withdrew her hand from the knob, and was about to pull out some paper when Jerome said, "No, let me do it." He had knelt in front of her, but she had closed her legs, saying, "Stop that! That's sick! What's wrong with you tonight? Jerome, you're one sick child. Stop! Leave my pussy alone." But he forced her legs apart, and wedged his forearms under her buttocks so as to lift her a few inches above the seat. He pulled her forward and, fighting the push of her hands, forced his mouth upon her piss-wet cunt and proceeded to lick every drop of liquid off her flesh until a change in the smell and taste of that flesh had informed him that her cunt was entering a different state. Meanwhile, Lavonne kept protesting and pushing against his head, saying: "Stop, Jerome! You're making me angry. You never forced me before. I'm not going to give you any of this pussy for a long time." But her voice sounded like she was simultaneously laughing and crying through her words, and Jerome did not stop, and then, suddenly, her hands stopped pushing, and, moving to the back of his head, pulled him in with such force that his air had been cut off. Jerome was gasping and his knees began to hurt but his lips and tongue did not waver in their duty. Then Lavonne thrust her pelvis violently forward. (What was she trying to do? Break his jaw?) And Jerome felt, in her whole body, that vibration that he knew so well and that thrilled him so.

Who? Who had been the master? And who had been the slave?

"Jerome, I wanna go home."

A rude awakening, even though he had not really been sleeping. Immediately he realizes four things: one, his mental trip had given him a royal hard-on; two, at the sound of Beatrice's voice his dick had instantly deflated; three, he has blown his act-as-a-pimp program to bits: and four, be doesn't feel like driving all the way to the Bronx.

"Beatrice, it's after one. By the time I get you home, it'll be after two. By the time I get back, it'll be after three. Give me a break! Can't you go to work from here?"

"Well, she replies," I did go home after work and change my clothes, so I suppose I can sleep here. I guess I'll be perfectly safe," she adds with a touch of sarcasm.

"I'm sorry if I haven't been a very good host. You see, I haven't gone out in quite a while. I broke up with someone and it left me... well... fragile, I guess."

"You wanna talk about it?" Beatrice says, leaning forward.

She seems like a good listener. Jerome is tempted. Being a rather solitary person, he's never had an opportunity to empty his heart about it. He decides not to do so: although he has failed in his program, there is still a chance, if only he can metabolize more of that damn alcohol. Certainly, to talk about Lavonne would negate any possibility of saving the night.

"Aw, it's okay. It's something I gotta work out by myself."

"Well, then let's talk about something else," she proposes out of boredom.

"Like what?"

"Oh, I dunno, how about current affairs? I'm a freak for current affairs. Where would we be without the cold war? Up the creek without a topic."

"How about you and me. Let's talk about you and me."

"You and also me, or you-and-me?" she asks, tracing the hyphens in space with her finger.

"You and me," he replies, indicating the quotation marks with two fingers of each hand.

"Jerome we've only met a few hours ago and, frankly, so far it hasn't exactly been rainbows and fireworks. So there ain't much to talk about."

"I'll admit we don't have much of a past, but we might have a wonderful future."

"I'm not much for thinking about the future and I don't like to bring up the past too much either. I'm a *now* person, Jerome. I guess it's one of my limitations. I'm a prisoner of now."

"Well then, let's talk about now. The you-and-me now of tonight. What brought you to Georgia's Peach – say, isn't that a dumb name for a bar?"

"Yes, it is. That's why we just call it the Peach. What brought me to the Peach? I guess it was the time of the month."

"Wha...?"

"Well, you see, Jerome, we women are cyclic creatures, in tune with the rhythms of nature: the tides, the seasons, the suicide of lemmings, the swarming of locusts, and the New Hampshire primary elections."

He is surprised to find her so bright and witty: it hadn't been his initial impression.

"Well," she continues, there comes a time each month when your body is invaded by the Kotex Devil. It does terrible things to you, and just as it leaves, it shoots a blast of hormones at your pitheal gland." (*Pineal*, Jerome corrects her inwardly – *or it is pituitary*?) "And you're left with a raging fire in there – or at least I am – and that's what brought me to the Peach."

"And as dumb luck would have it," Jerome segues, "you chose me or I chose you. Say, who chose who anyhow? Did you pick me up, or did I pick you up?"

"The seating arrangement did the choosing. The place was jammed and the only seat left at the bar when you came in was next to me."

"Ah, but, my dear, had that not been the case, and had I spied you in there, even if you had been escorted by a three-hundred-pound black-belt gorilla, I would have found a way to get to you, as you were by far the most charming and ravishing."

"Sure, sure, Your enthusiasm is evident. Look, Jerome, you got lucky... if you wanna use the luck. You sat next to a chick that was in the mood, okay? I figured: this guy looks alright... seems to be nice and all that. Look, you don't have to marry me. You don't even have to love me. Just treat me decent. And don't worry, I take the pill, I'm very careful about that. It's a freebie, Jerome, a freebie. Fun and relief, without responsibility."

Without responsibility, Jerome repeats inwardly. That reminds him of a few nights before. He had been sitting at some bar – not the Peach – when a pretty woman sat next to him. He noticed that she brought a drink with her, and that her eyes kept flitting back-and-forth, glancing alternately at him and at some indeterminate spot across the room.

She spoke first: "I dunno about men these days. I been sitting here a good half hour an' not one guy has offered to buy me a drink. Times must be tough. Finally I had to buy one myself, it was getting embarrassing. I guess chivalry is dead, hey?"

"You can have the next one on me," Jerome said without paying much attention to her.

She kept talking, finally involving him in trivial conversation. Halfway through the cocktail he had bought her, she said, "This place is creepy. Why don't we go somewhere nice."

"Well... I dunno," Jerome hesitated.

"Tell you what, you live alone? We could go to your place. You have anything to drink?"

"Well..."

"Look, I'm no whore or anything but I'm behind in my rent, so maybe you can help me out a little, okay? Can you spare thirty? You help me out, I'll help you out."

"I'm sorry but, but in a few minutes I gotta go someplace," he lied. "Maybe some other time, okay?"

"You just looked like someone that was out for some action. Well, nice talking to you."

And she wandered off to some other part of the room, toward some other guy, taking her drink with her.

And Jerome started thinking again about a question he had often pondered before: What is a prostitute really selling? Oh sure, she sells sex. But then, so do many "nice" girls in their dealings with men; so do advertising firms; and so do Hollywood and the whole entertainment industry. So, besides sex, what is it that the whore is selling? Perhaps, the opportunity to feel superior? To dominate? If the poor girl were unfortunate enough to be dealing with a psychopath she might even be selling her pain, disfigurement, or life – for thirty bucks. But none of these explained the difference between venal brides and prostitutes. And, then it hit him: responsibility – or rather, freedom from responsibility. A prostitute sells sex without responsibility – sex now, with no thoughts of tomorrow – and that explains why sexual prostitution (there are other kinds) was more prevalent among women than men: women have an umbilical cord between themselves and their sexual responsibilities, and thirty dollars cannot cut that cord. Can you imagine a man saying to a woman: "For thirty, you can fuck me, and then you can forget about it. You will not be held accountable for any aftermath." The man would be laughed out of the bordello! Oh sure, women sometimes neglect their children; sometimes abandon a newborn at a church doorstep. And these days, there is always the availability of abortion. Still, for thirty, or fifty, or even a hundred bucks?

And then Jerome thought of the cases – not that rare – when a prostitute gets pregnant and has a child. Does the child agree to sell freedom from responsibility for thirty dollars? There's always a fly in the ointment!

Beatrice is not a prostitute (in fact she is the very antithesis of a prostitute) yet, what she is offering is the same thing a prostitute sells: sex without responsibility, actual or implied; a now thing, unconnected to past things and future things. And the thought is a bit of a turn-off, because with it comes a feeling of emptiness.

"Yoohoo, Jerome. You here?" She is waving her hand in front of his eyes." Next time you go, take me with you, it must be fun out there."

"I'm sorry, I was thinking... Say, here's an idea," he gushes impulsively, "let's play spin-the-bottle like when we were teenagers."

"How can we play spin-the-bottle with just two people?"

"Easy. Think of the bottle in the middle of a circle. If it points in your half, you kiss me; if it points in my half, I kiss you."

"Silly! I have a better idea: lets play strip poker." She winks mischievously.

"Yea. Ah... but I so seldom play cards, I don't have a deck."

"Too bad."

"Say, I got a better idea than your better idea: let's play strip poker with imaginary cards."

"How's that?"

"Simple. You think of a hand, I think of a hand – you gotta be honest now – ready? Think of five cards."

"Okay, I got it." "What you got?"

"Get ready to drop your pants, Jerome: the ten of clubs, the ten of hearts, the ten of spades, the ace of spades, the ace of diamonds. A full house!"

"No way. You're cheating."

"How's that?"

"You can't have those two aces, 'cause I got four aces and the king of spades. My hand beats your hand anyway, and for cheating you get double penalty. Come on, take off two things."

"This game ain't gonna work out. I dunno why I let you talk me into this."

"A deal is a deal. Take off two things and then you can quit."

"Okay, if you insist."

She lifts her skirt and reaches under as if to take off her panties. If she is trying to arouse him, it might work: Jerome feels a slight tremor in his gonads. "April fool, fool." She laughs as she releases the skirt. She bends and removes her two shoes. "One, two. Satisfied?"

Jerome shuffles through his record collection. He is looking for Ellington's *Night Train*, a tune often used by strippers. He finds it and plays it.

"I've heard that tune," she says.

"Yeah, it's *Night Train*. It's a good number for strippers and go-go dancers. Since you got a start, I figure you might want to continue. Ever done a striptease for someone?"

"No, I'd feel stupid."

"Why? You got a nice body. It's just me an' you here. I won't tell, and I promise I'll still respect you in the morning. Come on, there's nothing wrong with it."

"I know there's nothing wrong it. It's just not me. I wouldn't feel comfortable."

"Look, I'll show you how. After I make a fool of myself maybe you won't be so shy."

Jerome starts his striptease act. Initially he intends to be really seductive and arouse both of them with his gyrations and divestment, but the clown in him irresistibly takes over. Every pose is exaggerated; every bump-and-grind is awkwardly magnified; his eyelids flutter; his tongue lasciviously licks his lips. One by one, the buttons of his shirt are passed through the slits (is she getting the symbolism?); then his left arm is denuded and he caresses his bare shoulder; finally, his right arm is freed, and Jerome swings the shirt in a wild circle over his head. With the last chord of the tune he throws the shirt at Beatrice's feet. She is laughing and applauding. "More, more! Take it off!"

The next number is slow and romantic, and Jerome is wondering if he should continue the caricature by – as they say in go-go clubs – working the floor. Instead, he takes Beatrice by the hand and pulls her up from the coach. He wraps both his arms around her and starts a slow, sensual dance. She likewise embraces him: her hands feel good on his naked back. He insinuates his right leg between hers, and exhales so that she can feel the hot air on her cheek and ear. The dancing becomes less and less active until they are merely swaying without moving their feet. When the tune ends, she disengages herself.

"Jerome, I gotta get some sleep. Where do I sleep?"

"In the bedroom, where else?"

He takes her by the hand and leads her to the bedroom. He turns the light on and adjusts the dimmer to get a kind of semidarkness.

"Are you going to join me?" she asks.

"Hm-hm."

He strips down to his shorts. He is debating whether to take those off also, but he notices that Beatrice has kept her underwear on, and he decides to do likewise. It is warm in the room. He discards the comforter: a muslin sheet will do. They slip under it and lie side by side, not awkwardly, but a little stiffly. Jerome reaches for the alarm clock on the night table.

"What time you gotta get up?"

"How long does it take to get to Broadway and

23rd from here?"

"That's easy. Take the F train at the corner. Takes you one block away to 6th and 23rd. Fifteen minutes on the train; another fifteen waiting – just to be safe."

"Alight then, I'll get up at 7:30."

"Mind if I set it for 6:45?" Jerome asks.

"Why so early?"

Jerome merely smiles.

"Oh, I see. You're one of those guys that wake up with a hard-on. You guys like it so much in the morning. Me, I like it when I go to bed. Makes more sense: it relaxes you and then you just drift to sleep."

"I know but, you see, when I drink – and it doesn't have to be that much – I become a sexual cripple. I'm real sensitive to alcohol that way. But by tomorrow morning...

"Leave it for 7:30. If you wake up earlier, you can wake me up."

Silence, except for the ticking of the alarm clock, every second, on the second. Jerome closes his eyes, but he is not falling asleep. Then, he hears a gentle rustling noise, and he feels, through a vibration of the mattress, a slow movement. A hand slips under his shorts. Again he notices how comforting her touching feels. The hand massages the whole genital area gently, playing with his pubic hair, stroking his penis, softly squeezing his scrotum. After a few minutes of this, the hand becomes more peremptory as it clasps his penis firmly and begins a deliberate stroking motion. He can feel the beginning of an erection. Without saying a word, Beatrice repositions her body and slips his underpants off. (He helps her by raising his buttocks off the mattress.) She retracts his foreskin and deftly licks the glans. Jerome's dick is half hard now and she engulfs it within her mouth, her lips encircling it like a ring on a finger. Her whole head is bobbing, looking for that metaphysical rhythm. Ah, now she's doing something! He knows her intention: to harden that cock in her own self-interest. It might work. Jerome is on the verge of moaning and saying things like, "Yes, baby, suck on that thing, oh yeah, you're doing it good," when she focuses on the head of his cock and applies a strong suction. But like many uncircumcised men, Jerome has a very sensitive glans. The sensation is too acute. It almost hurts.

He wants to tell her to return to the previous mode, but instead he gently pushes her head away and says, "Let *me* do it to you now." They change position. Jerome deftly parts her hair. He brings his lips to within a few inches of her pussy-lips and stops, letting his fingers do their exploratory work first. He feels no great enthusiasm for the task but, knowing himself, expects that he will warm up to it. Thank heaven for mouth and tongue: best guarantee against sexual embarrassment ever invented. Forget about saving face. The most important thing is to save dick on those not-so-rare occasions when one has drunk too much; or has had his confidence weakened by rejection, dispute, disappointment; or when Nerve, in its notorious unpredictability, is simply not up to it. Women are lucky that way: as long as the mind is aroused, the body will follow suite. With men, it's different: one can wake up with a cast-iron penis, yet feel no arousal; and then one can want it so badly he could cry, yet be burdened with an organ that has the consistency of vanilla pudding. Slowly Jerome's face sinks in the confluence of her belly and her parted and raised thighs. The first contact of his tongue with her labia is pleasant. Beatrice's pussy is clean but not oversanitized: there is a fertile wetness, a pleasant, musky aroma, and a slightly pungent taste. Jerome settles down to a workmanlike rhythm, and she responds like a good dancer. She reaches down and cradles his head in her hands, caressing the short hair at the back of his neck. It feels good. With his lips, he fishes for her clitoris. It is not very prominent but he locates it. He sucks it in and lightly clamps it between tongue and teeth. He shakes his head quickly, but carefully, from side to side, like a dog trying to pry a choice morsel from a bone. She neither moans nor cries out, but he can hear her breath quickening. He returns to his original rhythm. Shortly, the taste of her secretions changes to a sharp saltiness: a state-of-cunt message. Although he has neither felt a spasm nor heard any exclamation, he knows that he has accomplished his mission.

"Thank you, baby, that was good," she whispers. Within a few minutes she is fast asleep.

IX

Jerome is wide awake. He feels fidgety, but restrains himself, not wishing to wake Beatrice. Carefully he slips out from under the sheet and rises. He tucks her in, almost affectionately, and walks out the bedroom toward the kitchen. He notices a door slightly ajar on his left: Bobo's room. What is that door doing open? For months it has been kept closed. Jerome has entered the room only a few times.

For no particular reason he pushes the door fully open and enters. He switches the light on. Although the furniture is still there, the room looks bleak and empty. The radiator has been turned off months ago. The room feels cold, almost clammy. It has the aura of a dead person's room. Jerome can feel a constriction of his throat. He blinks a few times.

There are a few of Bobo's things left. On the day after the funeral, Lavonne, in a fit of desperate rage, had gathered all the child's clothing, toys, books and was about to throw out the lot for the sanitation men to pick up, when Jerome, who had just arrived from work, pleaded with her to save at least some of the stuff. She relented, and together they picked a few items. The rest was discarded. A few days later, Lavonne, somewhat more tranquil by then, thanked him for that. When they separated, she took with her most of what had been kept.

But Jerome insisted that some of Bobo's possessions be left where the child had spent the last eighteen months of his life. After all, who, with the possible exception of his mother, had loved him more? And who, except for Lavonne, would grieve more, and longer?

And so, on the wall are a Superman poster and a few of Bobo's crayon drawings; on the dresser is a framed photo of the boy, holding a baseball bat at the ready, and wearing a New York Mets cap and his Sunday smile; in the top right drawer are a bunch of pictures: Bobo alone, Bobo with Lavonne, Bobo with Jerome, Bobo with Jerome and Lavonne, Bobo with the folks at Bibleway Church; in the middle right drawer are a few articles of clothing: a sweater, a pair of jeans, even some underwear; on the floor, in a corner, are a pair of shoes and a ride-on toy roughly in the shape of an automobile; on the bed – or rather *in* the bed – is Bobo's favorite teddy bear. The bed itself had been made by Jerome the day after Lavonne left. He noticed how desolate the mattress looked, with its alternating stripes of blue and gray, and he went to the linen cabinet and took the one set of Bobo's bedding left, and he made the bed, trying to make it look as much as possible like a real bed made for a real, living little boy, and he tucked in the teddy bear, as if inviting Bobo's spirit (if there is such a thing) to stop by and rest there on its peregrination in the space of the dead (even if perhaps that space only existed in the minds of the living).

One thing that both he and Lavonne had refused to keep was any newspaper clipping about the accident. "Four-Year-Old Run Over By Bus," read one headline. "Horrified Mother Watches Bus Crush Child," read another.

It happened during rush hour, just after five. Lavonne had picked up Bobo at the nursery school. They were across the street from the apartment waiting for a green light. With one hand Bobo was holding on to his mother and with the other he was holding a plastic baseball. Somehow he dropped the ball and it rolled into the street, in front of a bus that was also stopped at the traffic signal. In an effort to retrieve the ball, Bobo broke free of Lavonne and took a few steps which brought him directly in front of the bus, so close that – due to his short stature and to the fact that he was stooping to pick up the ball – the driver was unable to see him. At that moment, the signal turned green, and the bus started, immediately crushing Bobo under its front wheel before Lavonne could react. The child died instantly – thank God for that.

Jerome came from work a little later than usual that night. He was surprised to find the apartment empty, but otherwise he noticed nothing amiss. (In a city inured to tragedy and accustomed to dealing with it perfunctorily, the traces of such events quickly evaporate in the interest of business-as-usual.) But then the phone rang – a ring that still reverberates in his head – and a police officer told him of the accident and informed him that Lavonne was at King's County Hospital, being treated for shock.

At first, no tears and no cries. Just a barely audible "Thank you officer," and an indescribable numbness, along with the feeling that the bright hues had suddenly been sucked out of colors, as though dark grayish lenses had suddenly covered his eyes. And Jerome knew then that the world would never again be the same, and that he, Jerome Dubinski, would never be the same. And then his eyes welled up and he felt that same spasm in his throat that he is feeling right now.

He had driven to King's County emergency room and waited half the night before being allowed to see Lavonne. Only then had he cried as he clasped her in his arm, their tears mingling in the interface of their cheeks. He had talked the doctor into letting her go with him. The physician had given him two pink pills and a prescription to fill in the morning, along with an admonishment to make sure she took the medication. During the ride back home, they hardly spoke and he noticed that she also seemed numbed. At first, he had thought this due, at least partly, to the effect of medication, but later he was to realize that some of that numbness would stay for a long, long time.

It was Jerome that made the funeral arrangements. Boy, had he hated that! Especially the little white coffin. "That's what's standard; everybody chooses that," the funeral director had said. And from that moment he has felt a loathing for white rectangular solids. That damn white box had burnt a hole in the retina of his eyes and left a lesion somewhere in his brain. Is there anything more pathetically sad than a small white coffin?

Jerome feels anger welling up inside his chest and in the pit of his stomach: the residue of that initial anger he had felt during the days following the accident. Anger because the world is made up the way it is, so that little children who have done nothing to deserve it and who are dearly loved by someone can be snuffed out, just like that. Anger because he, Jerome, felt cheated, since he had not been there, had had no chance to intervene, no chance to prepare himself for the tragic event, no chance to hold Bobo's head or hand as one would imagine a parent doing with a dying child – and he was a parent, damn it, much more than Bobo's father had ever been. He had even been denied the opportunity to see and touch the child for the last time, since, owing to the disfigurement of the corpse, the coffin had been kept closed. And Jerome felt an irrational anger at Bobo himself – the kind of rage a mother feels after saving a child from the consequences of its own foolish actions: running into traffic; choking on an object introduced into the mouth; playing with a knife, the stove, an electric tool.

Damn little pickaninny! What business did he have leaving like that with no warning? Didn't he know how it would torture his mother; how it would devastate the man who had loved him as much as any biological father could love his own flesh and blood? Didn't he know what it would do to the relationship of these two?

And mostly, Jerome felt anger toward himself – anger and guilt. What if he had come home early that day, instead of late, and had picked up Bobo at school? They would probably not have been at that corner, at the same time as the bus, at the same point in the red-green alternating of the light. What if he had not bought that fucking baseball? What if? What if? What if? And ultimately, what if he had never met Bobo, never altered the trajectory of his life, never perturbed the flow of *his* River. Of course, he had worked out all these hypotheticals logically, and he had come out clean. He had done right by Bobo, and by Lavonne. And then, if you bump into someone on a busy street; and because of that bump that person loses a step in his progression; and because of that lost step that person is hit by a truck a few blocks down the street; and that person dies: are you responsible for his death? Are you guilty? Of course not, no more than you deserve a medal if some action of yours has caused someone to miss an airplane, and that airplane later crashes. We are a social animal, and we are constantly bumping into each other and changing each other's life trajectory – each other's River.

Jerome understood all that, and yet, the thought bothered him – and still bothers him – that if he had not gone to the funeral of Harold Johnson's mother; that if he had not tried to meet Lavonne; that if he had not offered her a ride in his car: Lavonne would still be working at the nursing home, and singing gospel music in the Bibleway choir... and Bobo would still be alive. That thought will always bother him.

For Jerome had loved Bobo with a father's love, and the child had responded. Wouldn't go to sleep without Jerome's goodnight kiss on the cheek. Wouldn't finish his vegetables unless Jerome fed them to him ("Open the door, here comes the choo-choo: Whoo-oo-oo"). Wouldn't play his toy drum set unless Jerome accompanied him on saxophone. Boy! He would look at Jerome and beam such a smile – like Jerome would have done had he sat in with Charlie Parker, king of bebop. (Well, in Bobo's eyes, Jerome *was* Charlie Parker.) And Jerome valued that smile as he might have a review in *Downbeat* magazine, or a standing ovation at Carnegie Hall. So many fun things they had done together. Like boxing with the red father-and-son boxing gloves. ("Take it easy, Jerome, he's only a child." – "Ah, come on, he's a boy, you gotta toughen him up a little.") Like horse rides, and wild-bucking-bronco rides – when Lavonne wasn't looking. Like playing baseball... .

No, not baseball. The thought of the two of them playing baseball could never be a pleasant, bittersweet reminiscence, not since the accident, since it was the dropping of a plastic baseball that had triggered that accident. Jerome had started to smile faintly while remembering all these things, and now he feels sorrowful again.

He sits on the bed, pulls out his handkerchief, and wipes his eyes. He is quietly sobbing. He feels foolish. *Dumb bastard! You got a woman in your bed, just waiting for you and here you are, crying in the next room. Stupid asshole!*

He reaches for the ride-on car. He rolls it across the floor back-and-forth between his right and left hand. (How many times had he pulled or pushed Bobo in that car!) The repetitive, hypnotic motion calms him: the sobbing stops, the throat relaxes. He replaces the toy in the corner and walks across the room to the dresser. He opens the middle drawer on the right and takes out a blue shirt. He brings it up to his cheek. He is trying to feel Bobo by feeling the garment. He sniffs it, trying to detect a faint whisp of an odor. *Bobo's gone, buddy, forget about it*. He folds the shirt, replaces it in the dresser, straightens out the other garments, and closes the drawer. He returns to the bed and lies on it, staring at the ceiling. How many times, in the last six months, has he thought about it – Lavonne and him, after the death? Well, here goes again. And it won't help. He won't make any more sense of it this time. Why? Why hadn't he been able to nurse Lavonne back to soundness with words and hugs and touchings, and with just being there and caring? As great as their sex life had been before, why had he not been able to use that magic wand of his to prod her back on course?

It was that numbness that they both felt, but that had been deeper, more permanent, and more destructive in Lavonne. That numbness had been like a thick gooey gel that had permeated their space and impeded that intimate physical and emotional contact that had been natural and effortless before. Yet, time and caring should have washed away that gel. But that didn't happen.

It is difficult for Jerome to reconstruct that period. Communication between them had waned to such a degree that there is now little to talk or think about. After the tears they shared while in each other's arms, at the hospital, Lavonne had hardly wept at all. At the cemetery, however, as the coffin was being lowered into the grave, she sobbed quietly, she gripped his hand, digging her fingernails into his palm, and looked at him with the look of a floundering swimmer saying with his eyes, "Save me, save me, I'm drowning!" Jerome squeezed back against her hand and thought,

"Yes, I'll save you, baby. I'm here and I love you." But he had not saved her. The drowning swimmer had slipped through his grasp and disappeared. He had never talked about River to Lavonne. (How does one talk about River, and Nerve, and Higamus, and Hogamus?) But it was in River – in her own personal embodiment of River – that Lavonne had drowned, and was still drowning. (One can spend a lifetime drowning in River.)

One night he had been surprised to see her drinking a beer – in fact, two beers, since there was an empty bottle on the floor. She had not gotten drunk – on this, nor on any other occasion – but Jerome had thought it a bad sign. There were others: without becoming slovenly, she had shown less care about how she dressed, did her hair and nails, cooked, and how she performed her share of the household chores. She stopped going to choir practice.

But it was in bed that the change had been most pronounced. Of course, out of respect for her and for Bobo, Jerome had done no more than hug her and give her brotherly kisses until a few days after the funeral. When they resumed making love, Lavonne seemed passionless. At first this had not worried him too much. He remembered how reserved she had been the first few times they had done it, and how intense her loving had suddenly become after the third or fourth time. (She had later explained that, at first, it felt funny, making it with a white man; but that after seeing how he was with Bobo, she had found it easy to relax and "let it all hang out.") So he had not worried: her fervor would return shortly.

But it never did. And soon Jerome's passion began to weaken. He would have to touch himself in order to induce an erection. And then, in the middle of the act, he would feel his hard-on beginning to fade, and he would have to think of other women in order to maintain it. While copulating with Lavonne, Jerome had fucked women, big and small; tall and short; black, white and Asian; passively submissive and aggressively bitchy; heavily made-up and *au naturel*. He had fucked them in every position known to man or beast, using every orifice of their bodies. He had wedged his prick between huge tits and sucked small tits with inch-long nipples. He had even penetrated the rectum (the only no-no that Lavonne had ever enforced) of large women with huge asses and of skinny girl with bony ones. But at the last second, just before the excruciating rapture of ejaculation, Lavonne would retake possession of her body, and it would be between her loins that he would deposit his sperm. And it was Lavonne's rib cage that his arms would enfold; her cheek that he would kiss; and it was in her ear that he would whisper, "Was it good for you, baby? You gonna sleep good now."

But then, one night, he had fantasized his old friend, Felicia, the warm and good-natured whore from Boston, and Felicia had lingered past his climax, and it was in her belly that he had come, and it was her body that his arms had embraced. When, finally, Felicia had evaporated, Jerome had felt a great sadness. Lavonne too was evaporating. Her lithe brown body was slipping through his arms and, though he still loved her, there was nothing he could do. It wasn't just the sex – the sex thing was just a symptom – it was the world of Jerome and Lavonne that, deprived of its critical mass by the departure of Bobo, was crumbling silently. Jerome kissed her very tenderly, caressing her head with both hands, and he had said "I love you" with voice almost breaking. His eyes had filled with tears and Lavonne felt the wetness. She said, “What’s wrong Jerome? You crying?” and he answered, “It’s nuttin’, baby, I must have something in my eye, I dunno. It’s nuttin’.”

From then on the dissolution of their bond accelerated. They never fought – hardly even argued. When Lavonne started smoking, Jerome, very surprised, wanted to say something, but did not. When she bought a small bottle of gin, he made no comments. When she started leaving late for work and taking too many days off, he only said, “Don’t overdo it, You could lose your job.” Yet, through it all, he did not stop loving her, nor, he still feels, did she stop loving him. But perhaps it was a different kind of love ... And sometimes, love is not enough.

One thing she had started doing perturbed him considerably, but here again, he did not protest. She had acquired the habit of saying things like, “You’re white, you wouldn’t understand” or, “It’s a black thing, how would *you* know.” During the good times, she had never mentioned race or color in the context of their relation. (Well, one time, while making love, she had cried out, “Oh yeah, baby, jam that big white dick into me.” He had been both excited and unsettled by the exclamation. He almost retorted, "Oh honey, that white dick just can't get enough of that gorgeous black pussy," but he held back. It's one thing to dig the contrast between his skin tone and hers, to find exciting the sharp delineation of her dark brown body against the lightly colored sheet, to take pleasure in the soft cushion of her beautiful fleshy lips; and quite another to talk of white dick, of black pussy, of black girls' well-rounded asses – even in the throes of fucking. At any rate, Lavonne never said anything like that again.)

The realization that it was over soon settled like a dense fog over his heart, but Jerome had been unable to make any decision or initiate any action. He could not even consider asking her to leave. Where would she go? Who would look after that broken-winged bird? He had almost decided to leave her the apartment – with the furniture – and go find himself another place, when Lavonne had told him, matter-of-factly, leaving no doubt that is was a *fait accompli*, that she had gotten a job in a Boston Hospital. And four days later, just like that, she was gone. He drove her to the bus station, put three fifty-dollar bills in her hand, but she gave them back to him. "I'm alright, Jerome, I got enough. Don't worry, I'll be okay." He helped her with her bags. With the last kiss, she said, very softly, "I love you." And he, unable to speak, said it with his eyes and with a nod. He's glad that those were the last words she had spoken to him.

And she was out of his life. Not out of his mind, not out of his heart, just out of his life. Since then, not a word, not a letter, not a phone call. He has heard rumors, through one of her ex-coworkers, that she was doing fairly well at the job, but that she had developed some bad habits: smoking, drinking, perhaps worse. "I never would have believed it," the person said, "not Lavonne, not the Lavonne I knew."

Jerome raises himself and sits on the edge of the bed. He is wishing for Lavonne to be well, to be at least a little bit happy, to find someone or something. His eyes fall again on the picture of Bobo. With the startling suddenness with which ideas, once released from the crucible of the unconscious, impinge upon consciousness, Jerome perceives the solution – or rather what might have been the solution, because now it is too late. What does a coach do when a player is injured? He sends in a substitute. What do parents do when an only child dies? They make another baby. Jerome is astounded at his stupidity: the thought, obvious as it now seems, had never entered his mind. Stupid ass! Through the ages, babies have been the final answer to human disaster. After the Peloponnesian war: a baby boom. Upon Hannibal's return to Carthage – elephants and all: a baby boom. After the pest: a baby boom. After two world wars, the sex-starved soldiers and their horny wives hurried to the bedroom: again, two baby booms. In this case, what was needed was a mini baby boom – a one-baby baby boom. All he had to do was tell Lavonne – not ask her, but *tell* her, the way a doctor does not ask, but *tells* – to stop taking the pill and to make, with him, another brown-skin baby. Another Bobo – well, Bobo could never be replaced, but in time, certainly, the new child would have restored to River a strong, confident, purifying flow. Such a simple and obvious solution! And Jerome, stupid clod, had never thought of it! Well, it's too late... too late... too late.

He is tired now. He stretches and yawns. He smiles sadly at Bobo's picture, clicks the light off, closes the door, and returns to his bedroom. Beatrice is sleeping soundly. He slips under the sheet and, careful not to wake her, he gingerly places his body next to hers. He is tired. He is sleepy. He is sleeping.

X

He had not expected such a huge crowd at the park. He is also surprised at the number of blacks in attendance – and not all of them young radicals either. Many middle-aged establishment type blacks are there also. That's good. The oppressed whites have gotten some of the message across to the black majority. He looks down at his chest and reads the words imprinted on his T-shirt: *White and Beautiful*. Just a few years ago he wouldn't have dared wear that shirt – not out of fear, but out of a lack of pride and confidence. Just a few years ago he thought that being white was not as good as being black. Just a few years ago he thought that whiteness was a burden; and he remembers wishing, on occasion, that he had been born black. But that was before the civil rights surge. Now the downtrodden had leaders, and these were making a difference.

On his left, about twenty yards away, is a young black woman. How pretty she looks! And how pleasant and kind. There is an air of open frankness about her.

She also is wearing a printed T-shirt. If he can inch closer he will be able to read it. "Excuse me, sir..." "Sorry, ma'am." He can almost make it out now. Ah yes: *One nation, undivided, with freedom and liberty for all*. Now that he is closer, he can discern her features more clearly. She has a well-shaped head. He can see that because she is wearing a short afro. Looks damn good on her, too! She seems to be furtively glancing back at him. *I think she's looking at me. Why not? Best looking whitey 'round here! You'n me, baby, we could make beautiful music. I bet if she could hear me blow some white soul on my tenor sax, she'd dig me*. She is not wearing any makeup. Doesn't need any either: she has a beautiful face. Her even, brown complexion reminds him of a terra-cotta bust of an African princess he had seen in a museum.

Unconsciously, he has drifted even closer to her. There is a hiatus in the activities on stage: they are getting ready to introduce the principal speaker. It is his opportunity to close in on her and make his move. Damn, he would really like to meet her: she looks so nice, and pretty, and interesting. A few years ago he would not have dared, out of a lack of confidence. Now he has the confidence, but his newfound white pride and ethnic consciousness is erecting other barriers. The brothers might think he was selling out. He himself might think he was being a bit of a traitor to his race. In spite of recent gains in status for his people, he would still be the beggar, while she would be the noble dispenser of goodwill and fairness. He didn't want that. I won't join the club that way. That's the easy way. *And you, my dear, as much as I like you, will have to find another way to prove your passion for justice and your egalitarianism.* If only it were the other way around – if she were white and he, black – then he would certainly try to meet her, because then he would be the noble one – the disinterested one.

"I have a dream today," blared the loudspeakers. The main orator has started his speech. Jerome's heart skips a beat. What a voice: deep and sonorous, and with a vibrato as poignant as Sidney Bechet's on soprano sax. Jerome's chest is swelled out with pride and confident determination. We will overcome, yes. "I have a dream," continues the great man, "that one day every valley shall be exalted, every hill and mountain shall be made low, the rough places will be made plain, the crooked places will be made straight." – *Yes, there's a lot of work to do*, thinks Jerome, *but we can do it*. He looks toward the beautiful black woman, her eyes are riveted on the white man at the podium; her mouth is partially open; her whole face is glowing with excitement. Jerome is sure that she is feeling some of the same emotions he is feeling, in spite of her privileged background. "From every mountain side, let freedom ring." *Yes*, reflects Jerome, *and let freedom ring inside the mind and inside the heart, 'cause if it ain't there, it ain't*. The white orator is building to a climax: "Free at last! Free at last! Thank God almighty, we are free at last."

People are weeping, cheering, laughing, or just standing still – transfixed by the magic of the moment. Jerome is overcome with emotion. He wants to see what effect the speech has had on the black woman. He glances in her direction, but she is gone. He stretches on tiptoe, looks to the right, looks to the left; she is gone. The crowd in its confused shifting has swallowed her. Too bad, but what the heck, let's get on with it, there's work to be done.

XI

Jerome wakes from his dream. He is lying on his back, motionless, staring at the ceiling. That was a weird dream: up was down, right was left, and black was white. He will have to think about that one. Already, it has given him some insight into the hearts of black people, and perhaps, into the feelings of Lavonne. Now he can discern overtones he couldn't hear before when Lavonne said things like, "You're white, you just can't understand." Again, he flashes into awareness that irrational guilt he still feels: that it was partially his fault that Bobo had died, because if he, Jerome, had not intruded into his life, the child would still be alive. Certainly, Lavonne must also have felt guilty. More than he. After all, it was her who had been in charge of the boy at the fatal moment. And then, sometime during the ensuing days, she may well have thought: if I hadn't started with a *white* man, this wouldn't have happened. From this thought to the feeling that Bobo's death had been a punishment for her ethnic disloyalty would be but a small step – and

Jerome knows how resistant to rational analysis such feelings can be. Perhaps the death of Bobo was not the only cause of the estrangement. Perhaps it had only been the trigger. Perhaps it was the combined weight of that tragedy plus that other something in the back of Lavonne's mind that had destroyed the relationship. Oh well, he'll never know. And even if he should, sometime in the future, have a *tête-à-tête* with Lavonne, he could never ask.

But if that was the case, then the break-up might have happened anyhow – eventually – even if Bobo had not died. It was not just a matter of dumb luck! Jerome sees the whole story in a different light. He prefers it that way. It's a little less sad, and the sadness is easier to take. With understanding comes resignation, and with resignation comes relief. Some emotional weight has been taken off his shoulders. Already he can feel his breathing become easier and deeper; he can feel a lessening of that gnawing feeling in his solar plexus. River is flowing more freely. It will take him to sunnier valleys, to happier places.

His eyes are heavy once again. For some time he hovers between sleep and wakefulness, until a vibration in the mattress stirs him out of that state: Beatrice is moving. He looks out the window: a hint of dawn is washing the night sky. His naked body gravitates towards Beatrice's naked body. His right leg crosses over her left. His foot lodges between her partially parted limbs. His right hand slides over her abdomen until it reaches her pubic hair. His fingers massage that area in a circular motion. Her pelvis is tilting slightly back and forth in rhythm.

Jerome rolls over on his right side. His left hand finds one of her breasts. He plays with her tit and with her nipple. He pinches her nipple between thumb and forefinger. He tightens his grip and gives her just a hint of pain. He twists the nipple clockwise: just a little more pain. She does not protest, but her breathing quickens. Jerome can smell her morning breath. What the heck, his is probably just as bad! He shifts position again. His torso rotates so that his mouth can touch hers. He gives her a lazy, wet, deep kiss. Beatrice's hand closes on his penis. Damn, she knows how to touch! Then her fingers fondle his scrotum and then she finds his testicles and gently massages them, one by one. Just to make sure, Jerome brings his left hand down to his penis:

Yes! Yes! Yes! A glorious hardness! An erection! A hard-on! A bone-on! Yes, that big dick is standing at attention and saluting. And there is already a wetness at the tip. Quickly he dips a finger into her vagina, and there too there is a wetness. A big stiff prick and a wet open cunt. What more do you want? He can feel the waters of River simmer into activity. Pretty soon he will be swimming into white water. Nerve is out of his torpor, the moody bastard. *Go ahead, Nerve, give me a hard time, be difficult. I don't care. I can take it.*

Quickly, he places his body squarely over hers. With no guidance from either his or her hands, his penis finds her orifice. At first insertion is easy – almost automatic. Then there is a resistance. Jerome establishes an easy to-and-fro fucking motion, but with every stroke he is pushing against the obstruction and penetrating a little deeper. At the forward end of each stroke, however, there is pain as his uncircumcised penis is struggling – as much against its own foreskin as against the offending constriction of her vagina. But his erection maintains its structural integrity, and Jerome knows that he will prevail. *Higamus is with me, I will not fail.* And then there is a breakthrough: he has entered into the inner chamber, and there is no more impediment and no more pain. Penis and vagina are merged into one well-oiled machine – piston and cylinder – and the internal combustion is humming. Jerome's rhythm accelerates. He feels free, yet he is aware that he couldn't stop if he wanted to – like a sky diver in free fall, free in space, yet plummeting willy-nilly toward earth. Jerome, also, can feel a weightlessness. In the mental space of feelings and sensations he is in free fall, and it is, as always, an indescribable thrill: the criterion by which other thrills are evaluated.

There is no need for experimentation or esoteric sophistication. Plain old missionary position, doin'-what-comes-naturally, foot-slogging, down-in-the-trenches, infantry fucking. It feels as through his prick were swelling, like dough raising in the pan, filling every little nook and fold of Beatrice's sweet cunt, foraging in there for every bit of sensation, aspiring every milligram of pleasure. He wants more. He invades her mouth – or rather, their mouths interpenetrate. He wants to meld his body and her body, his juices and hers, his breath and her breath, his moans and her cries, his pleasure and hers. There is too much voluptuousness for one person. The head of his cock is sending waves of pleasure into her body and mind, and she is vibrating in tune, amplifying those waves and reflecting them back to him. He wants more closeness still. To raise her crotch and to tilt her pelvis to a better angle, he places his hands under her buttocks. She wraps her legs around his body and places her heels firmly on his rump. She presses firmly, almost violently, in time with his thrusts, deepening his penetration into her. He feels a pain in his back. An exciting pain. A pain that hurts a little, but that magnifies his other voluptuous sensations. She is raking his back with her fingernails. It induces a shifting of gears: the rhythm accelerates; the moans and cries amplify. Jerome can feel and hear the rush of air past his ears: the free fall has reached maximum velocity. His cock is proudly crowing now! Nerve is the boss and Nerve loves it. Jerome feels the omnipotence that a musician feels, who knows that he is swinging as hard as anyone can swing, that every note is falling into place, that no error is possible. He can sense the climax approaching now. The sweet-and-sour sensation is pushing its way toward that small insignificant looking crack in the head of his cock. The rest of the universe is vanishing. Even his body and her body are obliterated by the intense sensation. That sensation *is* the universe. And it starts: thump-a-lump, thump-a-lump, cascade after cascade. Beatrice screams and throws her arms and legs upwards. He can feel his spasms and her spasms, but can make no distinction between them.

And the free fall ends in a gentle splashdown. Jerome is swimming easily in the warm water of River, which has swept him into a luxuriant lagoon. The water is clear and tranquil. Awash, water lilies, white and yellow, are smiling at a sky, clear and blue. The sun is shinning, bouncing quanta of light here and there off the slightest ripple. Ashore, there are trees and flowers and grassy hills. Bird songs can be heard. A pleasant odor, earthy, watery, and sweet pervades. Certainly, this is Valhalla – the Valhalla where Higamus dwells and rules.

They are lying side by side, not talking. Only their arms are touching. Jerome feels a strong, paralyzing, but not threatening tiredness overwhelm him. His eyes close and he drifts into an almost comatose sleep.

XII

Holly shit! It's 9:40. He's way late for work. Got to call the office. What will he say? Gotta think of a story. He'll call later. Where's Beatrice? Is she in the bathroom? Probably not: her clothes and pocketbook are gone. Why didn't she wake him up?

On the bed, where Beatrice had lain, he notices a sheet of paper. There is writing on it.

Dear Jerome,

Boy, you sure can sleep! (Other things too you can do.) I had to leave for work. I shook you a little but you didn't budge. Figured I'd let you sleep.

Thanks for an interesting night. It started sort of weird, but the ending made up for that. (You dog!) See you at the club sometime, I'm sure.

Love,

Beatrice

P.S. Do you still respect me? Ha-ha.

Jerome turns the paper over. Why didn't she leave her phone number? That's strange, the tenor of the note is friendly enough. Certainly if he had been indecisive and somewhat cold early in the evening, he had more than redeemed himself later. What's her last name? She said it at the club, but he has forgotten. Oh well, like she said, they'll meet again.

Too bad, though. He had started just wanting to get laid, had lost his focus, but had ended up really making love to her. Even if it had been mostly physical, there had been a togetherness after all – and physical oneness, for all its limitations, is not that common, and not that easy to achieve.

In one mere lifetime, you can't expect too many relationships like he had with Lavonne. He sits on the edge of the bed, elbows on thighs, thinking about Lavonne with a mind altered by the dream he had earlier. Perhaps there was something he had missed. Maybe if he had understood Lavonne's inner self better... Was it his fault? Had he been wrong in trying to meet her? In asking her to live with him? In assuming the fatherly responsibility for Bobo? Was it wrong to have loved the boy with a father's love? What could he have done?

What should he have *not* done?

He is trying to be difficult with himself, yet he comes out clean from his examination of conscience. It had been, in many ways a marvelous time. And he was proud of many things. Proud of the way he had not let the intensity of their sex life overshadow the other aspects of their union. It would have been easy to get lost in the passion, in the near-freakiness, but he had not permitted that to happen. He had never stopped seeing in her the Lavonne he had met at Mrs. Johnson's funeral. He had never let the great sex eclipse the friendship or diminish the respect. As much as he disliked religion – except for H'gamism, of course – he had never trivialized her involvement with Bibleway Church. (How often had he driven her to choir practice? And how many times had he dressed up on Sunday to take her and her son to the church?) And he had never tried to bleach either the mother or the child. He had loved her as a black woman, and him as a black child, always accepting and respecting their blackness. If, after Bobo's death, that negritude had surfaced in Lavonne, and had been a factor in their estrangement, that was neither his fault nor, probably, hers.

He walks to the kitchen and makes himself a cup of instant coffee. Better call Mary at the office. What the hell will he tell her? He knows what a bitch she can be. "Why didn't you call earlier," she will say. "How can I run an efficient office if people goof off like that?" He hates to lie, but he's going to have to make an exception. Got to think of an excuse. He is tempted to take the day off, but old Mr. Wilson is hospitalized with a broken hip and Jerome's got to bring him his welfare check: the old man really needs it. And then he wants to go with Lydia Harris to the Bureau of Child Welfare to make sure that the Morrisson twins don't get lost in the cracks of the system. He's sure their mother's boyfriend abuses those kids. Boy, would he like to see that asshole in jail! He'll call the office later, after he thinks of a story, but he'll take a shower.

Jerome likes to meditate while the hot water runs off his back. This morning he is thinking about how fortunate it is that humans have such a lousy emotional memory. We don't forget the dead, but we forget the pain of the bereavement. We don't forget World War II, but we do business with the Germans and the Japanese. We don't forget old lovers, but we stop pining for them. Already, the emotional edge around his mental image of Lavonne is beginning to lose its bitter sharpness. Oh sure, he will never forget her; he will always love her in some way; but soon he will hardly pine for her. Still, perhaps someday they will meet again. Perhaps someday he will have the opportunity to do something nice and helpful for her. He would like that, yes. Be well, Lavonne, be well.

Last night, he took a giant step toward a renewed freedom. Jerome is singing I'm *Back in the Saddle Again*. The old cowpoke is back in the West. Look out fillies, my six-shooter is loaded. He had taken a chance and it hadn't worked out like he had hoped. But, what the heck, he is ready to take more chances. Now to get dressed and go to work. Hogamus time. Time to take care of business.

As for Bobo, that won't be so easy. Strangely enough, it is Bobo's memory, and the pain associated with it, that is more stubbornly ensconced in his mind. Jerome will always have an empty spot in his brain – a hole just big enough to hold the picture of a small white coffin. He'll just have to live with that. He'll just have to build a wall of endorphins around it, so that most of the time he will not be aware that it's there.

Like Yogi Berra said, "It ain't over till it's over."

But then, when it's over... .

It's over.

www.ingramcontent.com/pod-product-compliance
Ingram Content Group UK Ltd.
Pitfield, Milton Keynes, MK11 3LW, UK
UKHW040015200726
13854UKWH00001B/220

9 781412 065634